Forever Enough

THE MORE THAN ENOUGH SERIES

DONNA R. MADDEN

MARCUS HENRY
PUBLISHING

This is a work of fiction. All the characters, names, organizations, and events portrayed in this novel are either products of the author's imagination or are used fictitiously and are not to be construed as real. Any resemblance to actual events, locales, organizations, or persons, living or dead, is entirely coincidental.

No part of this book may be reproduced, or stored in a retrieval system, or transmitted in any form or by any means, electronic, mechanical, photocopying, recording, or otherwise, without express written permission of the publisher. v.2

Copyright © 2023 by Donna. R. Madden, all rights reserved.

Printed in the United States of America

Paperback edition ISBN: 979-8-9877343-2-2

eBook Edition ISBN: 979-8-9877343-3-9

Cover Art by: Champagne Book Design

Also By

The *More Than Enough* Series
These can each be read as a stand alone, but you will grow closer to the characters,
and there will be no spoilers if you read them in order.
Book 1: More Than Enough
Forever Enough (not a stand alone— continuation of Book 1)
Book 2: Your Love is Enough
Book 3: You Are Enough

To my husband.
You will always be
Forever Enough!

Forever Enough

Forever Enough is NOT a stand alone. It is a continuation of More Than Enough.

It is a story of betrayal and forgiveness and what a relationship sometimes needs to go through, and the growth those involved need to accomplish to finally get to their Happily Ever After.

Trigger Warning: Forever Enough focuses on the struggle two young people go through when trying to build a relationship because of a baby. Bad choices are made by both parties (Elizabeth and Brady) and there is one circumstance of cheating– off page. **If cheating is a no-go for you, DO NOT read this book. Skip directly to Your Love is Enough (Stacey's story).**

Prologue
July—Just After College Graduation

Brady's phone alerted him to an incoming text. He pulled into a parking space, put his truck in park, and glanced at his phone as he unbuckled his seat belt. The name of the sender caused him to look harder at the message, wondering what made a college friend he hadn't heard from since graduation two months ago finally text him out of the blue.

> **Trina: Hey, Handsome! How's your summer going?**

> Brady: Hey, Trina. It's been a while! Goin' great. Been working with my dad. Learning the business. How r things with you?

> **Trina: Awesome! Take a break and come visit me in Florida. Grab some guys. We have room.**

Brady paused, then quickly shrugged his shoulders. He and one of his fraternity brothers, Trent, had just been talking about heading to the beach before Trent left for Boston.

> Brady: Sounds possible. I'll see if I can get time off.

> **Trina: Let me know. Make sure it's soon!**

Brady pocketed his phone as he entered the doors of Warren Construction, the company his grandfather had started forty years ago. Now his dad runs it, and one day it will go to his brother Christian and him.

"Hold the door!" Christian ran up behind him and snatched Brady's phone from his pocket as he passed his younger brother to get into the office building first.

"What the hell, bro?" Brady shoved Christian and held his hand out.

"Relax. I'm just wondering who got your attention. I was yelling at you when you got out of your car. You were so into your text. You didn't hear me." Christian laughed, but he couldn't get past the security on Brady's phone and tossed it back to him.

Pocketing his phone, Brady rolled his eyes, walked into their shared office, and grabbed a Coke out of the small refrigerator. "It was that girl from college I told you about, Trina. She moved to Florida and invited me out. Told me to bring some friends. I think I'll ask dad for a week off. I never had a graduation trip yet, and Trent and I want to go do something before he leaves town. Might be fun." Brady sat at his desk and booted up his computer. They started every morning with a team meeting, and he needed to pull up the project he'd been working on.

"Isn't this the roommate of the girl you were obsessed with? What was her name?"

"Elizabeth, and I wasn't obsessed. Yes, it's her roommate" Brady glanced at his brother over his monitor. Okay, maybe he was a little obsessed. She was hot and fun, but he hadn't talked to her since graduation.

"That's not what it sounded like to me. You were in love with Elizabeth, yet she didn't want it to be just you two, and you were also with Trina. Y'all had an interesting relationship. I'm glad I've always had Deb. What you experienced was too much for me." Christian grabbed his tablet from off his desk. "Come on. Meeting's starting."

Friday came, and Brady and Trent were headed for Florida's panhandle. They had the week off and were looking forward to the white sands and blue waters of Panama City. Seeing Trina was an added benefit, for Brady at least.

"You said Trina had a roommate but didn't say who. Thinking it's Elizabeth?" Trent sat in the passenger seat with his arm out the window, enjoying the warm breeze blowing through the cab of Brady's truck as they flew down the back country roads of Florida, the Gulf of Mexico calling to them. They were making great time from Tennessee and should be pulling in soon.

"It's not." Brady glanced quickly at his college buddy and fraternity brother, then turned his eyes back to the road. "Trina said Elizabeth decided not to move to Florida. I guess she's in a relationship already and didn't want to leave him.

"Dude, have you talked to her at all since graduation?"

Brady shook his head, pursing his lips.

"That's it then? You're not gonna talk with the 'love of your life?'. You're just gonna move on like all your feelings never happened?" Trent sighed. "That's disappointing, brother. You gave up way too easy."

"Bro, you know how it ended. She made it clear we were done. I moved on."

Trent chuckled. "Yeah, okay. If you say so."

They rode on a bit longer, and finally, the bay came into

view. Salt air floated in the car windows as they crossed the bridge to the gulf.

After navigating the summer beach traffic, they finally found the condo. Brady pulled his truck into the parking lot of a three-story building and parked in an empty spot. They grabbed their bags and walked up the steps to the third floor. The smell of sand and salt air pulled them forward, and the sound of the surf filled their ears.

The door opened before they knocked. Trina's smile touched her ears, and her blue eyes were shining. "Brady, Trent, it's so good to see you."

Brady returned her smile, his eyes quickly traveling up and down her body. Trina was as gorgeous as ever. She stood in the door of her condo in a white lace bathing suit wrap, which easily showed a yellow string bikini underneath. Her blonde hair was highlighted by the sun, her body toned, and her long legs tanned. He wrapped her in a hug and breathed in coconut and mango lotion. Then, he and Trent were introduced to her roommate Malerie, a pretty brunette.

Trina ushered them into a tiny entrance way, which opened to a large room. Part kitchen, and part living room. On the opposite end was a glass wall with a sliding door leading out to a patio overlooking the beach. Brady took the short walk across the condo and out onto the patio. The white sand shimmered in the sun. Seagulls flew in the blue sky. There was a light breeze and calm water. He took in a deep breath of the salty sea air and itched to get down there and feel the sand between his toes—and see Trina in that bikini. His body reacted just thinking about her.

"For now, y'all can put your bags in the back bedroom, but we'll figure out sleeping arrangements later on." Trina's voice led Brady back inside. She ran her hand down his arm as he passed her.

Brady's eyes caught hers. He liked what he saw in their depths. "Which room's yours?" Brady asked as he took a self-guided tour of each bedroom.

"The front one."

Brady smiled and winked at her. Her room was small, just a small side-table, a double bed, and a closet. Big enough for them. He placed his bag on the bed and got out his beach towel. "Let's head down to the beach."

The sand was warm on Brady's feet, and the water was calling. He and Trent dropped their towels in the sand and kicked off their shoes.

He pulled his shirt off and sprayed sunblock quickly on his well-muscled torso and arms. "The water looks amazing."

Trina peered at him over her glasses. "I was thinking we'd just sit and talk for a bit."

Shaking his head, Brady grabbed her up, slung her over his shoulder, and ran toward the water.

Trent laughed and plopped down in the sand next to Malerie. "Later, dude. Have fun." He cracked open a cold beer, passing one to Malerie.

Trina squealed as she bumped along, her legs kicking and her hands swatting his butt. "Brady! Stop. Let me down."

"Whatever you say." Brady ran into the waves, kicking up sand and water. "Plug your nose. You're going in."

He pretended to toss her off, but instead, stood her up in the surf.

Catching her breath and holding tight to his arms, she glanced up at him, smiling from ear to ear. "You scared me. I thought you were gonna dump me in."

"What, like this?" Before she could do anything, he gathered her in his arms, went deeper, and fell into a coming wave, both going under.

She came up sputtering next to him and splashed him. "That was so unfair." She splashed at him and ran through the water. Brady on her tail. She was more agile in the water, but he caught her—several more times—each time tossing her farther into the surf.

Finally, she came up from the water and wrapped her arms around him. "Stop, please. I can't."

Her face lit up when she laughed. He didn't remember her being this beautiful. He held her gaze and searched. For what, he wasn't sure. A smile grew along the edges of his mouth. He was glad he was here, now.

He grabbed her hand and led her out of the water to their towels. They relaxed in the sun with a beer in their hands. The four of them talked and enjoyed the day.

The sun warmed Brady's skin, and he leaned on his elbows,

watching Trent and the girls playing corn hole. Trina looked tan and happy; her hair was sun-kissed blonder than usual. She smiled and looked relaxed, not like she did back in college. He could tell the beach was agreeing with her. Finally, she left the game, grabbed a couple of beers from the cooler, and joined him on his towel.

He opened the beer she handed him and took a deep drink, enjoying the taste of the cold liquid as it ran down his throat. "Florida seems to agree with you." He bumped his shoulder into her.

"It does. I love it here. I work, come home, watch the water, or come to the beach. It's a great life." She turned to look at him. "But It's gotten better."

Their eyes locked. A small smile slowly crept across Brady's face. His eyes searched hers and saw her lips part slightly. Brady's pulse started racing, and he reached up, placing his hand behind her neck. He pulled her face closer.

Their lips collided, and they devoured each other. The taste of salt, beer, and sun on her lips caused Brady's body to react until it needed more. His smoldering eyes searched hers. "Can we take this to your room?"

Trina nodded, a sly smile spreading across her face, and pulled him up, leading him quickly back to the condo.

Once they crossed the threshold, Brady grabbed Trina by the waist, turning her toward him. She squealed as she was caught off guard, her arms automatically wrapping around his neck to keep from falling over. He crushed his lips to hers as his breath left him. A moan escaped from her throat.

Lifting her into his arms, he carried her into her room and placed her on her bed. She was on her knees and reached for her bikini top. Brady grabbed her hands to stop her and he reached around to unhook the clasp. He watched with lust as her top fell to the bed.

His chest moved heavily as he stared at the perfection in front of him. His lips latched hungrily onto her mounds of flesh, and he sucked while she moaned his name. Finally, he trailed kisses up her chest to her neck, his tongue tracing a trail to her lips.

The kiss was deep. Their desire was evident. Trina pulled on Brady's swim trunks, and his craving for her became clear. Her eyes traveled up his body and met his eyes. "Brady. Please." She begged.

He took her. Hard and fast. Then lay together as the sun dipped below the horizon.

The week followed much the same way. Sand, surf, and sex became a daily habit. It was not something Brady complained about. With Trina, there was no commitment, no expectations. They were two friends who shared a physical attraction, and they knew how to please each other.

"So, you leave tomorrow. Will I hear from you soon?" Trina asked as she walked beside Brady, searching for shells. She stopped to pick up a small one and turned it over and over in her hand.

Brady didn't answer right away. As far as he was concerned, this was no more than how they treated each other in college. Just two friends having fun and making each other feel good. "I don't know. Is that what you want?" His eyes followed her.

Trina shrugged and kept her eyes on the sand, avoiding Brady's gaze.

Brady stopped, and his heart fell in his chest. The Trina he remembered didn't want commitment and knew he wouldn't give it. "Trina?" She continued to walk on. "Trina, stop." Brady ran the few steps to catch up to her and turned her to face him.

The tears shining in her eyes caught him off guard. "Trina, what's going on?"

She didn't answer, just shook her head.

Brady grabbed her face and forced her eyes on him. "Hey, I thought this was just fun, like it's always been. I like you, Trina, but ... I don't know if I can give you anything else."

Trina's hand wiped away his words. "I know, I know. I guess maybe I just thought that we both were ready for something more." She looked at him. Her eyes clear. "You're right. It was silly."

Brady didn't let go of her face. "No Trina. It's not. If it's what you want, we can see where this goes. I just don't want to promise you anything."

A smile broke through her lips, and she leaned in and kissed him.

The summer was over, and fall was beginning.

Brady was enjoying a much-needed afternoon with his family at his brother's house. His simple no-strings-attached relationship he had going with Trina all summer was getting ready to become more difficult, and he wasn't sure what to do about it.

Christian's boys were playing in the yard, and he and Christian were tossing a football back and forth. "So, how's Trina doing?" Christian asked Brady.

Brady tossed the ball and shrugged. "Well, you know. Good, I guess." He caught the ball again and tossed it lightly in his hands before throwing it back.

"When y'all were here last week, it seemed like she thought everything was going great." Christian caught the ball and walked toward Brady, ending their catch. "Something's bothering you. You've been off all night. What is it?"

Brady grabbed a beer from the cooler and took a seat on a lawn chair. He watched his nephews as they played. William, toddling around, pushing his bubble lawnmower, and Ben, with his three-year-old energy, on his little push bike, riding around cones. They're going to have a cousin. "These two are amazing." *I don't know if I'm ready for this.* He covered his face with his hands.

Christian sat next to him, smiling at his boys. William pushed his bubble mower to his dad and raised his hands in the air. Christian lifted him and sat him on his lap. "I agree. They are amazing." He kissed William on the head. "And sweaty."

Brady reached out and grabbed William's hand. Just let it out. "I talked to Elizabeth on Saturday."

Christian's eyes popped wide. "Elizabeth, from college? The love of your life, Elizabeth?" His eyes locked on Brady's.

Brady slowly nodded and turned his beer up, finishing it. He tipped the bottle upside down and watched as first one drop of beer fell to the ground, then another. He placed the empty bottle on the ground and turned toward his brother, his elbows on his knees and his head hanging, his eyes kept on the ground. "She's pregnant. I'm gonna be a dad."

Christian's mouth fell open.

Seeing his brother's reaction, Brady chuckled. "I bet that's what I looked like when she told me."

"Sorry, man." Christian placed William on the ground and patted him on his bottom. He toddled off to play in the sandbox. "I know you… how do I put this… had a creative relationship. Hell, y'all slept around. Are you sure it's yours?"

Brady nodded and breathed out a large breath. "She got pregnant in February. That's when we were dating exclusively. It's mine."

"Wow. You're gonna be a dad." Christian smiled. Slowly, realization dawned on his face, and he turned his full attention toward his brother. "Shit! Does Trina know?"

Shaking his head, Brady answered. "No. She doesn't. Elizabeth and I met at the Farmer's Market on Saturday. That's when she told me. We've been talking all week. I'm going to go see her soon."

Brady took a deep breath, held it for a beat, then blew it out. "I've got to tell Trina we're over. It's always been Elizabeth."

Chapter 1
One Year Later: Early May

"What the hell, Brady? Get out here and help me already!" Elizabeth waited for a response but got none. She slammed the door as she went back to cleaning off the patio. "Damn, you would think this was my place instead of his." She muttered under her breath as she pounded on the lounge pillows, a little harder than necessary, and lit citronella candles to help keep bugs at bay. He'd said he'd help her, but here she is doing it all herself.

"Hey, hey, hey. Someone needs to relax." Brady stepped onto the patio. He glanced quickly at his cell phone, sent a text, and slipped it into his back pocket.

Elizabeth placed her hands on her hips and sighed heavily as she shook her head at her boyfriend. "Really? I'm out here working my ass off for your housewarming, and you're inside on your phone? How is that fair?" She threw her hands up in frustration and stomped away from him. She was nervous enough about him moving into her town and becoming a bigger part of her and Grant's life. College graduation was a year ago, and their choices then were scattered. They were on-again-off-again more than any couple ever should be, and in between, they slept with others freely. They've been back together for six months since the birth of their son, Grant. Usually, Brady is all in and a big help, but what's gotten into him lately? He's moving here because they haven't been able to spend much time together, but lately it's seemed that his mind was always somewhere else. *God, I love this man, but really?... Breathe Elizabeth. You need to relax.*

She placed her hands over her face, taking in deep breaths. Her voice became calmer. "I can't believe how disrespectful you're being right now."

Brady grabbed her hands and brought them to his lips, forcing her to look into his eyes. "Relax. It's only our friends." He talked calmly, smiled his sweet smile, his eyes shining. "You are adorable when you're angry." He planted a kiss on her lips.

Elizabeth pulled away from him. "I just feel like sometimes I'm more into this relationship than you are. You've seemed so disconnected lately." She crossed her arms across her chest. "Like tonight. I came over here to help you, but I've been doing all the cleaning and prepping. You've been inside—on your phone." She grabbed his phone out of his back pocket. "What's been so important?"

Brady looked up at the clouds. "Come on, Liz. I was just texting your parents to make sure Grant was okay. I've gotta check in on our little boy. I miss him." He wrapped his arms around her. "And, yes, I've been a little distracted. Dad's throwing a lot more on me at work, and I want to prove to him I'm up to it." He pulled her close and lowered his gaze to meet hers. "Anyway, I'm gonna do all the cooking tonight. It's your job to just look amazing, and you're rockin' that." Brady's hands slid down to her ass.

Feeling the heat from his hands seep through her skirt, Elizabeth tried to suppress the smile that threatened to break through. She peered into his chocolate brown eyes, which were still laughing at her.

"I want to be mad at you, you know. But you checked on our boy. That's sweet." She loved how Brady took to being a father. He was a natural and never had an issue with baths or dirty diapers. Her body relaxed in his arms, and her anger disappeared.

"Yeah, well, you can't be mad at me. I'm the sweetest guy around." Brady's smile grew, and he placed his lips gently against hers. Butterflies entered her stomach as he deepened his kiss.

"And the hottest dad," Elizabeth whispered against his lips. She tightened her arms around his neck and answered his kiss, slipping her tongue into his mouth. Brady backed her on onto the patio couch, laid her down gently, and rested himself on top of her, filling his gaze with her.

"You're so beautiful." He brushed her hair away from her face and stared lovingly into her eyes. "Being here with you and Grant is the only place I want to be."

Elizabeth's heart thumped wildly in her chest, and she tilted her face against his hand, closing her eyes. "Texting you was one of the best decisions I made last summer. I love you, Brady." Overcoming her fear of becoming a mom and contacting Brady last summer was difficult. But she did it.

He smiled his wide, sexy smile that melted her insides. "I love you, too." Brady closed the space between them, and his lips met hers. The kiss was warm, yet demanding. Elizabeth's lips answered him, deepening their connection. He slipped his hand under her white denim mini skirt and quickly slid his shorts down.

Her need for Brady became overwhelming. Her pulse started racing as her body warmed. Being with him and having him inside her was all Elizabeth could imagine. Her hand went below his waist, and she curled her fingers around his shaft.

"Elizabeth." Brady's voice was hoarse as his breath sped up. He lifted her shirt, exposing the skin beneath it. He kissed her stomach and traveled up to her breast.

"Brady..." She pushed her body against him.

"Oh, Elizabeth... Yes." Brady's free hand went between her legs, and he felt how much she wanted him.

Elizabeth's eyes suddenly popped open, and she gasped. "Brady, stop! We're outside. What if someone comes early?" She wiggled her body, trying to break free of his grasp.

Brady pulled slightly away and looked into her eyes. "Elizabeth, no one is coming early except hopefully you and me." He held her gaze and lifted his eyebrows while his lips curled up. Elizabeth stopped trying to get out of his grasp; and a giggle escaped from her lips. Her laughter turned into a deep breath and a loud groan when he thrust into her. "Oh, Brady!"

"Hey, y'all made it." Elizabeth wrapped her best friend, Jessica, in a tight hug when she and her boyfriend Chad entered Brady's backyard.

"We would've been here earlier, but someone couldn't find the perfect outfit. Then her hair wasn't looking right." Chad rolled his eyes. "I don't know why she worries so much. She's beautiful to me."

"But you know what we think doesn't matter." Brady grabbed the case of beer from Chad's hands and gave Jessica a quick welcoming squeeze. "You'd think they were working so hard to get someone else's attention. Maybe we should be jealous." Brady winked at the girls.

"Whatever." Jessica swatted Brady's back as he turned away, amusement ripped from the guys as they went and placed the beer on ice. "Elizabeth, where can we put this food? Grams made her famous potato salad and brownies."

"Yum. I love your grandma's cooking. Let's take it in the house." Elizabeth led Jessica through the yard to the backdoor and into the small kitchen where the table and island were already overflowing with goodies. "It was so nice of her to make this for us."

"You know Grams. She loves to do for us, and she loves to cook for an army even more. She doesn't get to anymore, so she takes advantage of the times she can." Jessica placed the large pan of potato salad in the space Elizabeth cleared for her.

"Grams said she wants you to bring Grant for a visit. She misses seeing him in church and wants to see him before he starts walking."

Elizabeth placed the brownies on the dessert table. "He's only six months old. I think we have plenty of time before that happens." She picked a brownie from the pan and bit into it. "Mmm. These are so amazing. They're almost better than sex." She closed her eyes in fake ecstasy, shaking her head slowly back and forth, enjoying the deep chocolate flavors that exploded over her tongue. A picture of her lying on the patio couch flashed into her head. *Yeah, almost better*.

"Knock, knock." Stacey entered the kitchen and chuckled at the look of pleasure on Elizabeth's face. "I wondered what you thought was better than sex... I guess it's whatever's in your mouth."

Elizabeth glanced at Stacey and raised an eyebrow, then wrapped her friend in a hug. "I'm glad you made it. Did Steven come with you?"

Stacey wrinkled her face. "No. Let's just say that ship has sailed." She stopped the onslaught of comments from Elizabeth and Jessica. "It's for the best. I promise, and I'm fine. He wasn't the one. Time to move on."

Kristen, who followed Stacey, rolled her eyes. "Yeah, he so wasn't worth your time, Stace." She gave Jessica a quick hug, then turned to Elizabeth. "Your sex life hurting that much? I know brownies are good, but come on."

"So glad you're here, Kristen." Elizabeth's voice dripped with sarcasm. She scowled at Kristen as she offered the girls a brownie. "Maybe you should try one of Gram's brownies. They give Brady's abilities a run for his money, and I can tell you he's pretty good."

Stacey grabbed one from the pan and took a big bite. "Mm. I might have to agree with you. This is amazing."

"This coming from the single one who hasn't had sex in how long?" Kristen rolled her eyes. She picked a brownie off the tray, took a bite, and then quickly popped the rest into her mouth. She scoffed. "All of you need to think about getting new boyfriends. I don't need a brownie to substitute for good sex. I get that nightly." Kristen pushed her nose in the air, threw her shoulders back, and went to get a plate full of vegetables and dip.

Elizabeth placed the brownies back on the counter harder than necessary. *Why does Kristen have to be around when everyone gets together? If she wasn't dating Jacob, we wouldn't need to deal with her.* Elizabeth rubbed the back of her neck, feeling the start of a headache.

Brady came inside with the burgers and hotdogs, and Jacob and Chad followed close behind. He set the food down, and for a few moments, the room was completely silent. The guys shared a glance.

"Something's going on. You girls are never this quiet. What did we miss?" Chad asked as he picked up a brownie and placed the whole thing in his mouth at once.

Jessica slapped Chad on the arm, and she shook her head. He wiped his hands through the air. "You know what? Don't answer that. It's not important. The burgers are done. Fill your plates, and let's eat."

"Where's dill relish and spicy mustard? How do you expect us to fix our burgers without those?" Kristen looked around for the condiments.

Elizabeth's eyes shot invisible daggers before she threw open the refrigerator and slammed the condiments on the counter. "Your spicy mustard and dill relish. Anything else you'd like, your highness?"

Jacob stepped over to Kristen and placed his hand on her back. She twisted around to look at him but stopped abruptly when their eyes met. Her face softened just a bit, and she put her hands up. "This is good. Thank you."

"I'm gonna grab some drinks." Elizabeth stomped out of the kitchen into the garage. She paced the floor, taking deep breaths. "No one gets under my skin like that girl. She makes me want to scream."

"Hey, you, okay?" Brady stood on the top step. The door closed behind him, but she ignored him and continued to pace and breathe with her fingers grasped behind her neck. He grabbed her arm, turned her, and lifted her chin, forcing her to look into his eyes.

Elizabeth's hazel eyes met Brady's brown. She instantly felt her breathing relax. This man always had the ability to calm her. Ever since they met in college freshman year, just five short years ago. She combed her hands through his wavy brown hair, breathed in a deep breath, and felt her mouth curve upward.

"You good?" His stare sent a shiver of heat straight into her. She stood on her toes and wrapped her hands around his neck. "I am now. Looking in your eyes does that to me. They relax me. Everything about you relaxes me." Her lips met his. He returned a soft kiss, wrapping his arms around her waist.

"Kristen's been here for five minutes, and she's already getting to you. You've really got to learn to let her words roll off you like water off a duck." He dropped a peck on the tip of her nose.

"I know. As usual, you're right. I just wish Jacob had a different girlfriend. Having her around all the time is harder than being in the same room with him. He and I are good. She is just so... Kristen." Resting her head on his shoulder, she found herself staring at Brady's neck. She slowly started placing kisses on his soft skin, making her way up to his jaw.

"Well, at least you stopped calling her the crazy-whore-bitch. That's a step in the right direction." Brady's eyes closed as he stretched his neck and let out a soft groan. "What are you doing, Miss Parks?"

"Just taking my mind off my troubles." She whispered as she continued her kisses to his lips, where she devoured him. She walked him backward until his back hit his workbench. Her hands trailed their way down his chest to the button on his pants, and she felt a smile break across his lips.

"Do I need to remind you we have a house filled with our friends?"

Her eyes held his gaze. Their faces barely an inch apart. "If we stay in here long enough, maybe they'll leave, then I won't have to deal with you-know-who."

He kissed her again, a little softer, trying to relax and get his body under control. "Not likely."

Elizabeth broke away from him and let out a large breath. "Fine. Later, you'll get what I can't finish now." She winked at him and turned away.

His laughter filled the garage. He grabbed some drinks from the stack on the floor. "We need to bring something inside, so they don't just think you came out here to pace like a crazed maniac or take advantage of me."

"Kristen's here. They all know she drives me to be a crazed maniac. They wouldn't expect any less, and taking advantage of you—again, they wouldn't expect any less."

Brady shook his head and pushed her gently back into the house. "Let's fix our plates. Eating will make you feel better. And I have some chairs saved for us around the fire pit."

Chapter 2

Laughter and chatter rippled around the brick-sided fire pit when Elizabeth and Brady joined their friends. It was a perfect night to be outside. There wasn't a cloud in the sky, and the full moon cast a glow on the yard. Tiki torches added additional light, and music played on a wireless speaker. Elizabeth and Brady took the two empty chairs.

Elizabeth got comfortable sitting on the edge of her chair and picked up her burger, inspecting each side of it to see if she could open her mouth wide enough to get a good bite. Finally, she went for it and got lost in the greasy goodness. She found herself wondering what tasted better, the brownie earlier, or this burger now. "Either I'm hungrier than I thought I was, or this is the best burger I've had in a long time." She spoke through a mouthful of food.

Brady wiped a bit of mustard and mayonnaise from the corner of her mouth with his finger. "Mmmm. I love watching you open your mouth that wide. It puts some interesting thoughts in my mind about what could have happened in the garage." He sucked the mustard and mayo off his finger.

"You have a dirty mind, mister." She didn't take her eyes off him as she opened her mouth and took another seductive bite from her juicy burger, squinted her eyes in ecstasy, and chewed slowly.

"Later, sexy lady." He winked and gave her a peck on the cheek, then went back to his food.

"Are y'all done?" Chad huffed. "Remember, you invited us over."

Jacob laughed through a mouthful of food. "Yeah, we can always leave if you two need some time together."

"Sorry, I can't take my eyes off her." Brady wrapped Elizabeth in a hug and kiss that sent her heart soaring and her body reacting more than was appropriate at the moment. She placed her hands on his chest and reluctantly pushed him away.

Chad took a couple of beers from the cooler and pressed one cold bottle against Brady's bare arm. "Here, sexy. Cool yourself off."

Brady jumped and gasped for breath. "Damn, dude, that's cold!"

Chad chuckled and dodged a punch from Brady as he shuffled his way around the fire to Jessica. "They're playing our song."

Jessica's face beamed as he led her to the make-shift dance floor. They started dancing closely to the country song. Jessica, a petite girl, all of five-foot-one, was dwarfed by Chad's six-five build with girth to match. They were a perfect couple who had been friends for years but had been dating only a couple of months. He was a gentle giant who loved to joke around and was a perfect match for Jessica's sweet-as-sugar personality.

Jacob followed and led Kristen to the dance floor. "Make

room for us, buddy." Jacob hip bumped Chad out of the way and spun Kristen into his arms, her long blonde hair floating in the breeze. Jessica smiled and made eye contact with Kristen. Kristen's face shone with delight, like she was actually having fun.

"Beautiful, it's our turn." Brady offered his hand to Elizabeth.

"It would be rude to leave Stacey here by herself, and I want to finish my burger." Elizabeth turned toward Stacey, who grabbed the plate from Elizabeth's hands.

"Go dance. Your burger will be here when you're finished." Stacey pushed Elizabeth and sent a wink to Brady, who still had his hand out waiting.

"Fine." Elizabeth rolled her eyes playfully as she placed her hand in Brady's and pulled herself up.

He smiled and mouthed a thank you to Stacey as he wrapped Elizabeth in his arms. Good timing, too. Her favorite country song just came on.

They swayed to the music under the stars on the grass of the backyard dance floor. It was a perfect spring night, and Elizabeth was soaring with happiness. She found herself singing along with the words and laughing as Brady sang back the chorus.

When the song ended, he lifted his hand and gently caressed her jaw. "Elizabeth, we've been a part of each other's lives for five years, and I have loved you for what seems like forever." He whispered as his eyes locked onto hers. Her pulse raced, and she became lost in his dark eyes. He dropped his hands to his side, wiping them repeatedly on his shorts, and Elizabeth felt alone and empty without his touch.

"Is everything okay?" She studied him intently, trying to understand why he suddenly became so serious. She brought her hands to his face. "Hey…" It suddenly felt like the temperature outside increased.

Brady clasped her hands. His dark eyes smoldering with emotion. "This past year, since you told me I was gonna be a dad and we've been back together, has been the most amazing year of my life. You and Grant are the most important people to me. I want to be with you forever, Elizabeth. You are my world. You are my breath. You are my everything."

Her muscles froze, and her stomach started fluttering.

Brady dropped to one knee and pulled a sparkling princess cut diamond from his pocket.

Elizabeth's eyes grew wide, and her hands started to shake as they flew to her mouth. "Brady…" She stopped, not able to say anymore. Her heart felt like it would burst with happiness.

Brady grabbed her left hand. "I love you so much. Will you please do me the honor and say you'll marry me?"

Elizabeth fell to her knees in front of him. A huge grin was plastered on her face as she pulled him into a desperate, vice-like hug, and tears streamed down her face.

He hugged her back and laughed. "I really hope this means you're saying yes."

She pulled back from him, wiping her eyes. "Of course, yes." She kissed him with passion. She wanted him right here, right now, and made sure he knew just how much. He smiled widely and placed the ring on her shaking finger. She held up her hand to stare at the diamond and marveled at how it caught the light of the flames from the torches.

"It's beautiful and a perfect fit. How'd you know my size?" She looked at the man before her with amazement.

"I don't have to give away all my secrets." Brady gave her a sly smile and pulled her in for another long kiss.

"Excuse us, but you two aren't the only ones in the yard, you know. Please keep your clothes on." Chad raised his voice above cheers and clapping.

Chapter 3

Elizabeth's eyes popped open early the next morning, and her mind went immediately to last night. She brought her left hand up and stared at the ring on her finger, a smile creeping across her face and her insides warming. "One text changed my life. Brady, I'm so glad you stepped up. Even though I gave you permission to walk away."

Releasing a happy sigh, she got out of bed and walked over to her window, and sat on her window seat, enjoying the warmth of the morning light. Spring had come to the small country town, and with it, new life was blooming everywhere. Trees and bushes were waking up from their long winter slumber, and flowers were peeking up through the ground. "I love the spring. It's God's promise that we always get to start over, and this year, my life is about perfect."

The sounds of Grant babbling and cooing in his crib came through the baby monitor. She tiptoed to his room and opened his door a crack. He was busy watching the teddy bear mobile hanging over his crib, kicking his little legs, and waving his little arms, content in whatever his little baby brain was thinking.

Elizabeth crept into the room. He always woke up, so independent and happy. He must have gotten his morning-person trait from his daddy, because he sure didn't inherit it from her.

She leaned over the side of his crib and peered at him. He turned his head, grinned, and blew bubbles in greeting.

"Hey, handsome boy. Good morning."

Elizabeth picked him up and planted kisses all over his face and chubby cheeks. She laughed at his brief expression of shock and held him close, breathing in his soft scent of baby powder and shampoo. Then she laid him gently on the changing table.

"I missed you all night. Yes, I did." She tickled his tummy and got another smile in response, changed his diaper, and settled down in the glider to nurse him.

She closed her eyes as he fed and let her mind float backward to Brady's proposal. Thinking of him sent chills through her body, and the corners of her lips turned skyward. *I can't believe how much my life has changed in just a year. This time last year, I was ready to forget about college and the bad choices I made, and now I'm a mom and engaged to Brady. Sometimes, things have a way of working out for the best. Thank you, Lord, for your hand in our lives even when we don't realize you're there.*

Finding out she was pregnant was a shock. Luckily, she called a wrong number, and an amazing woman, Deloris Green, the director of the Crisis Pregnancy Center, helped Elizabeth make a choice she didn't think she was capable of—the decision to keep her baby and become a mom. There was no doubt in Elizabeth's mind that if she didn't miss-call the pregnancy center that day in June, Grant would not be in her arms.

Elizabeth opened her eyes and sighed a happy sigh as she stroked Grant's cheek and watched him nurse. Her vision became blurry. "You are the most amazing creation, little one. Becoming your mom was the best day of my life." As if he understood what she said, Grant stopped nursing and gave her a smile and laughed before he went back to his breakfast. Elizabeth giggled and wiped away a tear. "Guess what else! Your daddy is coming to see us today, Buddy. We have a big day ahead. He asked me to marry him last night. We'll finally be a family."

She was bubbling with excitement as she skipped down the stairs with Grant in her arms and joined her mom and dad in the kitchen. "Good morning, parents." Elizabeth sang. She kissed her mom on the cheek, and her dad on the top of his head. Her parents, Charlotte and Jackson, exchanged a questioning glance at her unusually cheery attitude this early in the morning.

Elizabeth settled Grant in his highchair, fixed herself a cup of coffee, and looked out into the backyard with the mug of steaming coffee in her hand. A pair of cardinals, male and female, were eating at the bird feeder. She couldn't tell if they were the same ones that were always there, but it didn't matter. She, like them, had finally found the forever love she had always looked for. Not just in Brady, but also in Grant.

Sighing contentedly, she took a seat at the table with her parents, where she had a cinnamon raisin bagel, a banana, and a glass of orange juice waiting for her. Her go-to morning meal.

Elizabeth hummed to herself and danced in her seat as she spread cream cheese on her bagel. "You know what amazes me, Mom and Dad?" Her parents met her eyes. "This time last year, my life was so different. I wanted to forget about school. I wasn't happy with myself and what I had become and was a depressed mess. Now I have this boy right here." She tickled Grant under his chin. He drooled chewed up cereal in response. She wiped the drool from his chin. "And I have the love of his daddy. Life is amazingly good."

Her dad tilted his head. "I am so glad everything's working out for you, Lilly-Billy. I love seeing you bubbling over with happiness. It makes my father-heart happy."

Elizabeth looked at her dad with gleaming eyes. "Thanks, Dad."

She picked up her orange juice with her left hand. The diamond ring on her finger glittered in the light pouring through the window. "Guess what." Elizabeth was practically bouncing out of her seat with anticipation as she wiggled the fingers of her left hand.

"Oh my gosh, Elizabeth. What is that?" Mom flew out of her chair, ran around the table, and pulled Elizabeth to standing so she could get a better look at the ring adorning her finger. "Tell me about this."

Elizabeth's dad stood up to look, as well. "What is this?" He held Elizabeth's left hand and showed her the ring, like she hadn't seen it yet.

"Brady proposed to me last night when we were all at his house." A smile lit up her features as her face glowed with happiness.

Elizabeth's face dropped, and she breathed out a small sigh. She placed her hands on her dad's arms. "I know, Dad. We've only been together for a few months. I know you have your concerns about us and our relationship. But, you like Brady. We aren't getting married only because of the baby. We love each other and want to be a family." Elizabeth paused and turned toward her mom, who gave her a small nod. She turned back to her father. "Yes, I know having Grant sped things up a bit, but I know this is how it's supposed to be. It's a good thing, Dad. It really is."

Her mom gathered her in a tight hug, tears running down her face as she rocked Elizabeth. "I'm so excited for you.

Breaking away from her mom, Elizabeth smiled, her eyes bright. "Thank you, Mom." She turned to her father. "Dad?" Elizabeth lifted her shoulders to her ears, making herself smaller.

Her dad studied the ground for a long second before a grin broke across his face, and he trapped his daughter in a bear-like hug. "You know I like Brady. He stepped up when he needed to, and he's been so good to the both of you and took a stressful situation and faced it head on. I'm happy for you both." Pulling away, he looked her in the eye. "And if it doesn't work out, he'll be the dumbest guy in the town."

There was a knock on the door, and Brady walked into the house like he was waiting for the perfect moment. "Well, can I guess that you all heard the news?"

Charlotte turned toward him. "Brady, come here." He

walked into her tight embrace. "Congratulations! We're so excited. And the ring is beautiful."

Brady's face beamed. "Thank you."

Jackson approached Brady and shook his hand, pulling him in for a hug with a strong pat on the back. "I guess a welcome to the family is in order. Congratulations! You have an amazing girl here, you know."

"I know, Mr. Parks. I know." He returned the handshake and hug, then turned to Elizabeth. "Good morning, beautiful." He leaned in to give her a quick kiss and a hug. "Hey sport." He placed his hands on Grant's head and gave his son a kiss.

"So, did you discuss a date?" Dad asked as everyone returned to their breakfast, and Brady joined them in an empty seat by Elizabeth.

"No, not yet." Elizabeth laughed and rolled her eyes. "I would love a small, simple fall wedding. Maybe here in the backyard. I don't know if we'd be able to get a wedding together by November?" She glanced at Brady and around the table. Her dream wedding didn't give them much time to plan. "I know that's quick. Like six months, but I really don't want to wait."

Brady shrugged. "That's your choice. I don't know what all goes into planning a wedding.

"A lot. A spring wedding would be better and would give us a year to plan it." Charlotte looked at Elizabeth hopefully. Elizabeth's shoulders slumped forward as she picked absently at her bagel. Charlotte sighed, knowing when she lost. "But, if you want a simple wedding, nothing too extravagant, I think we can put it together by November."

Jackson drank his coffee and added, "All I know is that weddings are a lot of money, so whatever saves me the most money is great to me."

The girls laughed at him, and Elizabeth squeezed her father's hand. "Well, Daddy," she said in her sweetest daughter voice. "It's a good thing I'm your only daughter, and you want me to have the wedding of my dreams, don't you?" She gave him a little pouty look.

Mr. Parks rolled his eyes. "Can we change the subject, please? Anyone."

"Well, you know there is something I wanted to ask you." Brady peered at Mr. and Mrs. Parks. "I was hoping to take Elizabeth and Grant to see my parents today so we can tell them the news, and I was wondering if you both could watch Grant for the night when we get back. I'd like to celebrate with my bride-to-be and keep her out all night. We won't be long tomorrow. I'll have her back by noon."

"What?" Her face heated. It was no secret that she and Brady have had sex—Grant was sitting there eating pieces of his father's banana—but still talking about spending the night together with her parents made her uncomfortable.

Her mom talked over her mug of coffee. "We'd love to watch the best baby ever all night. It'll be fun. You both go. You need some time for yourself. He'll go to church with us tomorrow, and we'll have fun spoiling him."

"Thanks, Mom." Elizabeth smiled at her parents. Then

turned to Brady and stood up, pulling him with her. "We'll be back tonight around five or six. I'll get Grant ready for bed, then we'll go."

Charlotte got up to clear away the breakfast dishes. "Y'all go and enjoy your family, Brady. When you get back, you can just drop off Grant and get out of here. He's so good, it won't be a problem."

They got up and helped clear the table. Brady took care of getting Grant ready to go while Elizabeth showered and changed.

Chapter 4

Brady pulled into the tree-lined driveway of the two-story brick house where he grew up, and parked behind a black SUV belonging to his brother, Christian, and wife Debra.

Elizabeth chuckled as she looked out the window. She loved the chaos of Brady's family. It was something she didn't get at her house being an only child, and her heart swelled as she pulled Grant from his car seat. Brady's nephews, William and Ben, had taken over the yard. There was a tiny tricycle and pedal car parked hap-hazard in the driveway, and balls and bats strewn all over the grass.

They let themselves in and wandered through a large sitting room, following the sound of family. Brady pulled Elizabeth into the sunny kitchen. The usual noise and excitement increased when they walked in. Grant got all the attention, and was quickly stolen by his grandma, while there were hugs for Brady and Elizabeth. Three-year-old Ben, Brady's nephew, ran to his uncle, and Brady swooped him up, throwing him over his shoulder. The young boy squealed with joy.

"Hey, girl!" Debra pulled Elizabeth into one of her signature hugs. All strength and love. "Here ya go." She handed her a freshly poured glass of wine.

"Thanks." Elizabeth took a large sip and side-stepped to make sure not to spill her wine, as William, Debra's one-year-old, came toddling toward his mom, a cookie held as high as he could hold it, as he was being chased by Toby, the golden retriever. Laughing, Elizabeth lifted her glass to Debra. "To chaos and family."

Debra expertly toasted Elizabeth, while throwing William on her hip, saving him and his cookie from being devoured by Toby.

"You girls can't drink that by yourself. You better pour me some." Joanna, Brady's mom, placed her arm over Elizabeth's shoulders and held her empty wine glass out for Debra to fill. Elizabeth smiled at the pretty brunette who had yet to show any evidence of gray hair and gave her a squeeze.

"It's great to see you, Joanna. What happened to Grant? I didn't think you'd be sharing him." Joanna was a wonderful grandmother. She loved on her grandbabies every chance she got and was always ready for fun.

"Yeah, well, Tim grabbed him up and said something about it never being too early to get used to a four-wheeler, so I decided to take advantage and come grab a glass of wine before you two finish the bottle." Elizabeth's eyes grew wide, and Joanna laughed. "You better get used to it. You are a boy mom now and a mom to a Warren at that. The Warren boys are all about being loud and getting dirty."

"Amen, Joanna." Debra lifted her glass in agreement.

Elizabeth relaxed at the bar with Joanna and Debra, who had a lap full of William. When the men came back into the kitchen, Grant was asleep in his grandfather's arms. Joanna jumped up quietly.

"Let's go lay him down to nap." She waved Elizabeth away when she got up to follow. "We got this."

Brady came up behind her, wrapping his arms around her shoulder and pulling her back to the bar. He kissed her cheek and whispered in her ear. "You ready to tell our news?"

"Yeah, when your parent's get back."

"What news?" Debra asked as she gave William a cookie from the jar on the counter.

He rolled his eyes at Debra and flicked his gaze down toward Elizabeth's hand. Debra grabbed Elizabeth's left hand; her mouth dropped open as she elbowed Christian hard in the gut.

Christian doubled over, clutching his chest. "What the hell, Deb?"

Ben came running into the kitchen. "Daddy said a bad word!"

Christian grabbed him up as he ran past and tickled his tummy. "The kid can't hear you tell him to clean up, but when I say one word, he shouldn't hear..." Ben squealed.

"Will you just hush and look?" Deb shook Elizabeth's hand toward Christian.

Christian put Ben back on the floor and let out a whoop of excitement. A smile filled his face as he wrapped Elizabeth in a hug. "Look at that! You finally realized how awesome we Warren men are." He wacked his little brother on the back. "Finally, gonna settle down. You go, Bro. I seriously can't believe you finally did it." He engulfed Brady in his arms and pounded him on his back.

"Okay, what did we miss? What did Brady do? Get arrested?" Catherine, Brady, and Christian's younger sister entered the kitchen with William close behind.

"Yeah, all that hollering almost woke up the baby. What's going on in here?" Tim asked as he and Joanna returned.

Christian kept his arm around Brady's shoulder. "Brady and Elizabeth are getting married."

The kitchen was filled with cheers and congratulations to the happy couple.

Catherine grabbed Elizabeth's hand and stared at the ring. "Oh, my gosh!" She looked up at Elizabeth, her eyes squinted. "I can't believe you actually said yes to that idiot."

Elizabeth's mouth dropped open as Brady grabbed up his little sister and put her in a headlock. "Hey, don't be mean, squirt." He rubbed his knuckles over her hair as she squealed and laughed.

"Okay, Okay! I give."

"That's what I thought." He let her go, and she had to catch her breath from laughing.

She leaned on her brother and wrapped him in a hug. "Seriously, bro. Congratulations."

"Thanks, sis." Brady gave her one last squeeze and a peck on her head before he let her go.

Brady's mom squeezed forward and wrapped Elizabeth in a hug. "Congratulations, Elizabeth, and welcome to the family and the craziness."

Christian stuck his fingers in his mouth and let go a shrill whistle, which got everyone's attention. "Thanks for calming down, everyone." Debra shoved him playfully, and he wrapped his arm around her shoulder. "I just want to say something." Everyone got quiet and gave him their attention. He nodded. "I remember years ago. Brady came home one weekend. We were out back drinking a beer, and he kept talking about this beautiful friend of his." Christian put friend in air quotes. "I asked him if this 'friend' was special. I'll never forget the look on his face. 'She's the one, man. Now she just has to realize it.'"

Brady punched Christian in the gut, his face an adorable shade of pink. "Dude, that was part of a bro-pact. You can't break a bro-pact." Christian leaned away from another punch, laughing along with everyone in the room.

"You guys and your 'bro-pacts.' Whatever. I'm just glad I'll have another sister. Two brothers are just too much."

Debra laughed and gave Elizabeth's hand a squeeze. "Congratulations for real. I'm so glad we'll be sisters. You and Brady make such a great couple, and it's about time he settles down."

Elizabeth liked Debra. Even though she was a mom of two young boys, she was always organized and prepared. The chaos of this family was second nature to her.

Elizabeth led Brady out of the room, looking for a little privacy and quiet. She pulled him to the front porch, wrapped her arms around his neck, and leaned into him, planting a long, sweet kiss on his lips. She gazed into his brown eyes, the same eyes as Grant's, as he gazed down at her.

"You really said that about me to Christian, all those years ago?"

"I told you I was smitten with you the first time I saw you. You took my breath away then, and you still do. Five years later." He tucked the stubborn lock of hair behind her ear and stroked his finger along her jawline. "I feel like I'm living in a dream, but if I am, I sure don't want to wake up."

Elizabeth stared at him, trying to see deep in his soul. "I don't understand why you never said anything. How were you okay with me dating other guys? Being with Trent, your best friend? If you would've said something, things might've been different."

"Or I could have scared you off altogether." He picked up her hands and admired the ring on her finger before he brought them to his lips. "I was just glad I had you when I did. I loved just being with you. If graduation didn't happen, who knows what we would've decided?"

"At least Grant brought us back together." She held his gaze.

His hands cupped her face. "I love you, Elizabeth."

"I love you back." They closed the small space between them, wrapping their arms tighter around each other. The kiss they shared was warm and loving. Sweet, yet demanding.

"Eww. Uncle Bwady and Elizabeth are gwoss!" Ben peeked out the front door.

They stopped their kiss and touched their foreheads together, laughing at the three-year-old who interrupted them.

Brady didn't move his eyes from Elizabeth. "Yeah, kissing girls is gross."

Ben came out and stood next to Brady. "Then why do you do it, Uncle Bwady?"

Brady held onto Elizabeth's gaze. "Because sometimes gross things are amazing." He gave her another quick peck and broke away. He caught Ben in a hug and swung him upside down over his shoulder. Ben screamed and beat his arms and legs, trying to get away.

"Time for lunch," Debra called from inside the house.

"Yay. Lunch." Ben's upside-down voice carried to her ear as she opened the door to allow Brady to carry him in, still kicking and screaming, hanging upside down.

Deb laughed quietly and playfully slapped Ben on the bottom as he passed by. "Shush. Your cousin is asleep. You don't want to wake him."

Brady and Christian went outside as soon as they finished their lunch and dessert to let Ben run and work off his sugar high. Christian handed his brother a beer as they walked to the back of the property with Ben running ahead, flapping his arms like a bird. Christian laughed at his son as he watched him, then turned to Brady and became serious. "So, are you sure about this? Marriage is a big step."

Brady gave Christian a side-glance and a slight shake of his head. "What, don't you think I'm capable of being tied down?"

"Not at all what I was thinking. I know you have feelings for Elizabeth, but what happened with that girl I saw you texting at work? It was Trina, wasn't it? Wasn't she the one you were with last summer right before Elizabeth? What's going on with that? Why were you texting her?"

Sighing deeply, Brady took a huge gulp of his beer and leaned against a large oak tree which stood by the pond in the back of the property. Brady watched Ben throw rocks and sticks into the water before he answered his brother. "Yeah, I don't know what the hell's up with her. No matter what I tell her about Elizabeth and me, she's not taking the hint. I told her she and I were over a long time ago. I told her I loved Elizabeth. She just doesn't get it."

"It's been a while since you saw her last, hasn't it? What, about eight months?" Christian squinted his eyes as his voice got louder. "Does Elizabeth know anything about you and Trina?" Seeing the interruption about to spew from his brother's mouth, he added, "Does Elizabeth know that you were with Trina right before she told you she was pregnant?"

Brady lowered his voice. "I never saw the purpose. Now Trina's talking about coming to visit her parents. Her dad's sick and her mom needs her closer. If that happens, she'll only be a short drive away."

Christian nodded. "So, tell me something. Did you tell her you were planning on asking Elizabeth to marry you? Does she know that at least?"

Brady's face fell, and he looked at the grass.

Christian let out a sigh. "Come on, Brady! Why haven't you? You want me to believe you're ready for one woman, yet you can't tell the other one the truth."

Brady looked into his brother's eyes, bringing his hands into the air. "I don't know. I'm gonna tell Elizabeth soon. I have to. Trina's gonna be calling her any day now. Trust me. Nothing more will happen between Trina and me. I love Elizabeth. It's only her." Trina was always trouble. Being with her last summer wasn't a good decision.

Christian placed his hand on his younger brother's shoulder. "I hope so, bud, but Elizabeth needs to know."

"Who needs to know what?"

Brady turned quickly toward the high-pitched voice of his sister-in-law and his eyes got wide and his pulse skipped a beat when he saw Deb and Elizabeth standing right behind him. He turned slowly to face his brother; his eyes closed into slits.

Christian walked toward his wife and laid his arm around her shoulder, pulling her close. He gave her a quick peck in greeting. "Not sure." He turned to Brady, his eyes shining, and called Ben to follow them. Ben ran past his parents again, his arms out flapping like a bird's, and he ran in circles back to the house. Christian and Debra laughed.

Brady gave Elizabeth a small smile. "Hey, Babe."

Elizabeth looked questioningly at Brady as she approached him. "Hi, yourself. What do I need to know?"

Brady gave an uncomfortable laugh as he sent his brother a frown and a tight gaze. "Oh, nothing important. We just have a big contract coming up at work and Dad is making sure we both stay busy. It's a great opportunity to show him what I can do, so my hours will be getting longer. It's not really a big deal." He laced his finger with hers and steered her back toward the house.

"Except that you need to be prepared to eat alone and be a single momma for a bit. They tend to get wrapped up in these big contracts." Debra chimed in and saw the look of concern cross over Elizabeth's features. "Don't worry, Joanna, Kristy, and I tend to get together a lot and do some girl and kiddo stuff. You'll have to join us."

Elizabeth smiled at her future sister-in-law. "I'd like that. Just let me know when you have something planned. Grant needs to spend time with his cousins."

Christian and Brady exchanged a look, then Christian followed the girls into the house. Brady leaned against the door and closed his eyes. *I've got to talk to Elizabeth soon. Things could get ugly if Trina says something to her before I do.*

Chapter 5

They finally got away from Brady's family and made it to his house before the sun went down. Brady stopped on the porch and unlocked the door. He turned to Elizabeth. "Wait here a minute, please?" He placed a quick kiss on her lips.

Elizabeth waited patiently for him to return, though she was confused as to why she couldn't just enter already. Finally, he ushered her through the doorway with a big sweep of his arm.

There was a congratulations banner hanging on the mirror, and a bottle of champagne on ice with two glasses waiting for them on the table. Brady popped the cork off the champagne, poured two glasses. He faced his future bride and handed her a glass.

Elizabeth stared at him, and her skin tingled. "You did all this before you came over today?"

He nodded his head. "Except for the champagne, which I just took from the fridge and put on ice."

"How did you know we'd be able to find a sitter?"

"Well, I figured your parents wouldn't care. But if, on the off chance, they did, we had my parents or my brother and Deb to fall back on. If none of them came through, he would've just had to be a good little boy, sleep in his crib, and deal with things."

"You have a crib here for him?" He only has two bedrooms, one being his office. "Where'd you put his crib?" Elizabeth wandered through the kitchen and noticed a desk in the corner of the living room. "You moved your desk down here?" She turned to him, and her eyes were wide.

"This will be our house soon, so I moved my desk down here to make room for his things. His room is nothing fancy, yet, but I wanted to have something so you both can come and stay whenever you want." He held his champagne glass in the air. "Anyway, here's to the most beautiful future bride on the planet." Brady tapped his glass to hers and they both sipped their champagne.

He took her glass and set them both down on the table. The look he gave her made her insides turn molten. He placed his hands on the side of her face and hungrily closed his lips on hers. Elizabeth's arms wrapped around his chest, and they kissed. It was a hot, demanding, yet gentle kiss. There was no rush. They had forever.

Brady reluctantly pulled away and played with a lock of hair lying on Elizabeth's shoulder. "I don't know if this is the right time. Please let me know if it's not, but I would love for you and Grant to move in with me. I want us to be a family, and I want you both here with me every night when I come home from work. What do you think?"

"Seriously? You really want us to move in now, before the wedding?" Elizabeth became still and her pulse raced. That's a big step. It's not just the two of them. They have a baby to think about. Maybe it would be a good idea.

Brady cupped her face, holding her gaze tight. "There's nothing I want more, except, of course, for you to be my wife, but I'll be getting that soon enough."

She loved his large, dark brown eyes and his perfectly chiseled chin. There was nothing she wanted more than for them all to become a family and move in together. "If it's really what you want, yes. We would both love to move in here."

"Good. That's settled. He covered her mouth with his and swept her off her feet, carrying her to the bedroom.

He set her down next to his bed, where the comforter and sheets were already pulled down, waiting for them. The soft glow from the bedside lamp cast deep shadows in every direction, and desire filled her body as she looked at the man standing in front of her. Her eyes wandered from his long powerful thighs, up to his firm, broad chest, and his muscular arms, to the deep brown of his eyes. The anticipation of what the night had in store shot a bolt of electricity through her body and down her spine, warming her from the inside out.

Brady kept his smoldering gaze on her as she slowly unfastened each button of her blouse, slipped the sleeves off her shoulder and down her arms, dropping it to the floor, exposing the white lace camisole underneath. Her breasts were pressed tightly together, adding cleavage. She could see Brady's chest rising and falling at a faster pace.

She gave a shy smile and slowly unbuttoned her skirt. When it hit the floor, she stood before him in her white lace strapless camisole and white lace thong.

Brady's eyes lingered on every part of her body, and he licked his lips like a hungry lion ready to devour it's kill. She slowly turned, showing him all views of her, yet making sure she kept her eyes on him the best she could.

He removed his pants and unbuttoned his shirt, fumbling over his buttons in his haste. Elizabeth sauntered toward him and finished the job. She placed her hands under his shirt, feeling the heat of his skin, and rubbed his hard, ripped chest. She lifted his shirt off his shoulders and down his arms slowly, making sure her hands never lost contact with his soft, warm skin. The entire time, their eye contact never wavered.

"Brady, I love you so much." She kissed him on his chest. He pulled in a sharp breath.

"I need you." She trailed her kisses up his neck. A groan escaped from Brady's throat.

She cupped his face in her hands. "I want you." She closed her mouth hungrily over his lips, pushing her tongue in to dance with his. His hands wrapped around her and gripped her ass, pulling her closer to him. Everything else fell away, and the world ceased to exist. At this moment, nothing else mattered but her and Brady. Their kiss deepened and became hungry and desperate.

She pulled away and took a second to catch her breath. "All the times we've been together, I've never felt this much for you." She couldn't stop the tears that filled her eyes and rolled down her face. "I feel like...."

He stopped her with a gentle kiss. "Shhh." He wiped away

her tears. "I think it's just our hearts finally getting to the same place as our brains. We were meant to be together. We know it now. You fulfill me in a way I never knew was possible. You and Grant are my life and give me purpose." He rubbed his hands along her back. "I'm so glad you decided to have this life and let me be a part of it. My goal is to show you every day how much you mean to me." His eyes bore into hers like they needed to see and know everything that was within her soul.

He kissed her gently. "Elizabeth…" He kissed her again. "I love you." He devoured her mouth. Holding the back of her head with his hand as he led his other hand around to cup her breast.

"This outfit is… Wow." He slid his hands down her sides, over her hips, and up her stomach. Finally, he stopped at her breasts and caressed them.

Her eyes closed as his hands traveled over her body. This felt so right. His hands molded her and her skin warmed. His mouth found her neck. He placed kisses there and his tongue licked a path from her shoulder to her cleavage. His hand pushed the lacy material covering her breast to the side and his lips skimmed over her flesh. Elizabeth sighed and a soft moan escaped from her throat.

As Brady closed his mouth over her sensitive breast, a shudder of pleasure ran down her spine. He nibbled and sucked, driving her mad. She stopped the magic between them by separating from him and quickly completing her strip tease.

Standing naked in front of Brady, she motioned for him to come closer while she walked backward toward the bed. She was the Pied Piper, and he went where she led. He grabbed her quickly, and they both fell on the bed as he held her tight. Brady kissed her neck. The stubble of his chin left scratches of desire and continued to her breasts where the softness of his lips made her draw in deep breaths.

She was in heaven. He was driving her wild and she couldn't wait any longer; she needed him to fill her now. Grabbing the sides of his head, she stretched up and crushed her mouth to his; he straddled her and leaned away, giving them both a chance to catch their breath. Her gaze traveled slowly down the length of his body and back up to his face. Their eyes met. This amazing man was hers, and in a few short months, he'd be hers forever. She closed her mouth around his as he filled her. She moaned as he pushed into her harder and harder. She kissed his chest and dug her nails into his rear as she shattered around him just before his explosion filled her.

Brady collapsed beside Elizabeth, and she rolled over and laid her head on his chest. She listened to his breathing and his heart beating beneath her. His heart was now hers. Soon to be forever. She smiled and kissed his chest.

Brady wrapped his arms around her. "I love you, Elizabeth. So much."

She moaned a response and was lulled to sleep by the beating of his heart.

Brady made breakfast the next morning—all of Elizabeth's

favorites: fresh fruit, bagels, juice, and coffee.

Elizabeth sat in her silky, white, lace robe, her hair wet from the shower. She studied him from across the table, a smile breaking across her lips. He looked sexier than ever in lounge pants, which sat low on his hips. He was shirtless, and his muscular torso was perfectly chiseled. His hair was also wet from their shared, steamy shower.

"You're too far away." Elizabeth lifted her foot, trying to reach Brady's chair under the table, but failed. He slid his chair closer and pulled her leg into his lap.

"We promised we'd get some food in our stomachs. Eat up." Breaking a piece of banana off, he leaned toward Elizabeth.

Elizabeth opened her mouth, and he placed the piece of banana on her tongue. She quickly closed his fingers inside and sucked on them lightly as he pulled them out of her mouth. She chewed slowly and seductively.

"Stop looking at me like that." Brady's voice came out low and husky.

Shaking her head, she slowly got up, went over to him, and straddled him. Their lips met. She felt him growing hard beneath her. She raised her body off him just enough to pull down his pants and set him free.

Brady laid his hands on her hips. "Liz, do we really have time for this? We have a baby to get back to."

She cupped his face, holding his eyes on hers. "We have plenty of time."

Slowly, she lowered herself onto him until he filled her. A moan escaped from his throat and she covered his lips with hers.

Chapter 6

"Hi, Dad. We're home." Elizabeth sang as she walked through the front door and enveloped her dad in her arms.

Brady quickly followed behind her and gave Mr. Parks' hand a firm, welcoming handshake.

"So, where's my boy?" She glanced toward the stairs. It was less than twenty-four hours, yet it felt like it's been forever since she's seen Grant. Her mom finally marched down the steps with an armload of baby.

Elizabeth took Grant from her mom's arms and cuddled him. His face lit up and her heart melted. It was difficult to comprehend the amount of love she had for this boy. Her heart was full when he was in her arms. Sometimes it was hard to believe that he was hers.

Brady hugged them both and kissed Grant, making him giggle. Elizabeth was surrounded by her men, and she knew she was ready to get a life started where they were together every day. Her heart swelled.

"Mom and Dad, thank you so much for watching him. We really appreciate it."

Elizabeth's mom sat down at the kitchen table with a cup of

coffee in her hand. "It wasn't a problem. We loved having him all to ourselves and want to do it more often. So, how did your family take the news?"

Brady and Elizabeth joined Charlotte at the table. "They were excited. It was a bit crazy actually," Brady answered.

Jackson placed a package of cookies on the table and grabbed a handful to enjoy with his coffee. He glanced from Elizabeth to Brady. He cupped his elbow and tapped his lips in thought. "Okay, what's going on between you two? I feel like you have something you need to tell us. What other surprises can you put on us? You have a baby, you're getting married..." He took a bite of a cookie and sipped his coffee.

Okay, Elizabeth. You aren't one to beat around the bush, so don't start now. Just come out with it. She took a deep breath and spit out what she had to say in one breath. "Brady asked me and Grant to move in with him."

Brady chuckled softly as his hands rubbed his neck. "Well, nothing like just blurting out an issue that might start an uncomfortable conversation."

Her parents sat with their eyes wide.

"Mom and Dad, we need to be together. We're a family. It was hard when Brady lived with his parents, and we only got to see him on weekends. Him moving here made it a little easier, but he still wants more time with Grant, and we want more time with him." Grant was getting fidgety, so she passed him to Brady. "We know it's gonna be difficult and will take time to adjust to each other, but we're ready and want to be together."

Her parents passed a look between them.

Her father shrugged. "We agree. We think it's a good idea. It's a big step, and there are a lot of pros and cons, but you're both adults, and most importantly, love each other." He stopped and took another sip of his coffee. "Promise me something, though." Elizabeth and Brady nodded. "You will talk to each other about everything and be there for each other, no matter what. That's the secret of a good long relationship." He reached out and grasped Charlotte's hand. "It won't always be easy, but as long as you remember, your love for each other is more than a ring, or words, it's also actions; you'll have a long and healthy relationship."

Oh, Dad. You're always the worrier. We love each other and trust each other. We got this.

Brady grabbed her hand and kissed her knuckles. "I promise, Mr. Parks."

"Call me Jackson, Brady. We're going to be family."

"Yes, sir."

Elizabeth watched as a look of respect passed between her two favorite men, and her heart swelled with pride.

"And start calling me Charlotte. And when are you gonna be taking my daughter and handsome grandson home?" Her voice gave a little and her eyes filled with tears. She reached out and held Grant's little hand.

"Mom..." Elizabeth jumped up and gave her mom a hug. "We'll just be a couple of minutes away. You can come by anytime, and we'll come visit so much you'll be sick of us."

"Well, Charlotte... Jackson." He tried out their names and shrugged. "Sounds weird, but I'll get used to it." They all laughed. "We were hoping to move some things today. I have a room for Grant ready, so we won't need anything from his nursery here. This will be his second home."

Jackson glanced at his daughter, and then his wife. "It looks like our daughter is moving out." He grabbed Charlotte's hand.

Charlotte smiled at him and reached for a napkin to wipe the tears from her eyes.

"Thank you both for being so understanding. I love y'all so much."

Charlotte sniffled. "We love you too, baby."

Chapter 7

Brady and Elizabeth settled into a comfortable routine. They had times when living together was difficult, and there were adjustments they each had to make. Simple little things, like Brady needed to work on rinsed the toothpaste out of the sink after brushing his teeth, he needed to remember to hang his bathroom towel on the hook instead of keeping it in a heap on the floor, and absolutely had to make sure the toilet seat was down after peeing. Dropping into a bowl of cold water was not Elizabeth's idea of fun, especially when it was dark, and she least expected it.

She had to remember to keep her piles of discarded clothes off the floor, store her makeup back in her makeup bag, and put away all her hair accessories.

Just like their life together, everything in nature also moved on and spring began to turn into early summer.

It was a gorgeous summer day, and Elizabeth and Brady were busy working in their yard. Elizabeth filled pots with red and yellow petunias and was planting yellow and burgundy gerbera daisies in the front garden. She stood back with her hands on her hips, admiring her work. The flowers added color and looked amazing.

Grant squealed in his playpen. "Really, buddy?" His toys were strewn all over the ground. "You wouldn't need to get so upset if you just keep them in with you." She placed them all back in the playpen. He squatted down with one hand on the side, picked up a block and threw it out again, giggling as he watched it lay on the ground. Elizabeth tried to act frustrated with this game but couldn't hold back the grin that spread across her face.

"I was thinking." Brady stood up and wiped the dirt on his gloves on the sides of his pants. "We haven't had anyone over since we've been here together. Why don't we have a bar b que?"

Elizabeth placed the blocks back in the playpen and watched Grant as he sat on his bottom and played happily with one of his toys. She slowly turned, making an inventory of their backyard, and nodded. "Yeah, I think that'd fun. We could give ourselves a housewarming. Grill out, have drinks, play some corn hole, and sit around the fire pit on the patio."

Brady looked around at the small backyard. "Umm, our fire pit isn't on a patio. It's in the grass."

"Well, I guess you'll have to get busy." God, Brady was hot. Even after working in the scorching sun all morning, sweaty and dirty, his chest glistening with sweat. Elizabeth sauntered toward him and wrapped her arms around his waist.

"Really?" Brady rested his arms on her shoulders.

"Yep. I found this cute and easy to build stone patio on the internet with a pergola over it. All you need to do is follow the directions, oh, and of course, purchase the material. I know you'll make it look amazing. Call Chad and ask him to come help." She stood on her tiptoes to kiss his lips.

He held her gaze. "It's just about impossible to say no to you. And you're right, a patio would really look good here. I'll take off early one day this week and get started."

What an amazing guy. I'm so lucky. Elizabeth's face beamed.

"I'm useless when you look at me like that. Miss. Parks. Your wish is my command." Brady laughed and pressed his lips against hers. She moaned when he didn't let up—taking the kiss even deeper, driving her crazy.

"Looks like someone wants something more right now. Too bad there's a baby needing our attention, and dinner. We may need to put this little make out fest on hold for now. In a bit." He traveled his lips down her neck to her shoulder blade, breaking it off when he heard her breathing become quick. "Baby needs us." Smiling and raising his eyebrows, he peeled himself from her grasp and went to pick up his son. Laughing at her over his shoulder, he walked into the house.

Elizabeth closed her eyes to compose herself. She sighed and rushed to the door behind Brady.

Chapter 8

"Hey, you. We're here." Jessica announced as she entered, with Chad following close behind, his arms filled with bags and cases of beer.

Elizabeth rushed to grab some food and bags and placed them on the counter. She gave Jessica a tight squeeze. "I'm so glad y'all are here. You can help me get this last-minute stuff done."

"Where's your man?" Chad glanced outside.

"He's dropping off Grant at his parent's house. They're watching him and Christian and Deb's boys tonight so we can relax and have good adult time and extra drinks without needing to be responsible."

Chad broke open his case of beer and placed the bottles in the ice bucket. He grabbed three when the women came back outside, opened them, and handed them out, keeping one for himself. "Here's to not needing to be responsible."

"For at least one night." Elizabeth toasted and took a big gulp of the cold liquid.

"What did we miss out on?" asked Brady as he entered the yard, followed by Christian and Debra. He hugged Jessica, then bent down to get a beer out of the bucket. He draped his arm around Elizabeth's shoulders.

Elizabeth stretched her neck to give his cheek a kiss. "Hey!" She squealed, jumping away. She pushed her chest out as her arms folded around her back. Cold, cold, cold. She tugged on her shirt, trying to release the ice. Several pieces fell, but she could feel others still there, stuck to the inside of her shirt, and melting against her skin. "Brady.... What... the ... heck.... Jess.... Help!"

Luckily, Jessica pulled out the remaining ice. "Asshole." She threw it at Brady's chest, trying not to laugh.

He wrapped Elizabeth in his arms. "Sorry, but I couldn't resist." He struggled to catch his breath through his laughter.

She pushed him away. "That was rude..." Her shoulders shivered, and a chill went through her body. "... and cold!" She hid her face in his chest to hide her laughter.

Brady took a swig of his beer and gave her a peck on her cheek. "That was worth it to see that shiver that just went through your body."

"You're such a pig!" Elizabeth swatted at him playfully.

Christian clapped Chad on the shoulder. "Anyway, what were y'all drinking to when we walked in?"

"We're drinking to not having to be responsible tonight and being able to get sloppy drunk." Chad lifted his beer in the air.

Christian held up a finger and went and grabbed two more beers. "I think we'll both gladly drink to no responsibilities." He gave a bottle to Debra.

"Thanks, Babe." Debra took a quick drink.

Elizabeth guided the girls inside to help her finish preparing the food, while the guys started a corn-hole competition.

"Who else is coming tonight?" asked Debra.

"Just y'all, and I invited my friend Trina. She came home from Florida to visit her parents. They don't live far from here, and she gave me a call yesterday."

"Is she the one who you roomed with in college?" Jessica asked as she finished dumping chips into bowls. She smoothed out the chip bags and placed them in the corner of the counter.

Elizabeth's eyebrows flicked up.

"For later, just in case there's extra chips, you have somewhere to put them."

Elizabeth nodded. "Okay, thanks. But, yeah, she is."

Debra froze as she was opening the package of cups. Her eyes flicked quickly to Jessica. The two girls held each other's gaze, their eyes wide.

Elizabeth looked between her friends. "Okay, y'all. What's up?"

Debra shook her head. "Nothing."

Jessica's gaze left Debra's. "Really, you invited Trina? Wow, if you're good with her being here, I'm interested in meeting her."

Elizabeth placed her hands on the counter. "Look, I know it might seem strange, but we've all grown up. What happened in college is in the past. She knows Brady and I are together, have a baby, and are engaged." Noticing the doubt in her friends' eyes, she breathed out a heavy breath. "Y'all. Trina mentioned there's a guy she's interested in. I promise, it's good."

"I hope so," Debra whispered under her breath.

Jessica shot Debra a quick look and took three shot glasses from the cabinet. "Well then, let's get this party started." She filled them with tequila and gave one to Elizabeth and one to Debra. They all took a shot of tequila.

Debra grimaced. "I think I'll stick to beer tonight. I can't handle that." She placed her shot glass in the sink. "Anyway, I guess we should head outside and see when the hamburgers will be ready if they've even started cooking yet. I'm getting hungry."

"Yeah, me too. Is there anything else you need help with, Liz?"

Elizabeth shook her head. "Nope. Everything's ready. Let's go." Jessica linked her arm through Elizabeth's, and they followed Debra out the backdoor. After just a few steps, Jessica stopped abruptly.

"What the hell, Jess!" Elizabeth yelled as she ran into her, knocking herself sideways.

Jessica had to put her hand up to stop Elizabeth from falling and gestured to the other side of the yard. "Who's that girl next to Brady?"

On the other side of the yard, Brady stood by the fire pit, deep in conversation with a pretty blonde.

Elizabeth's face lit up and her heart took a hard leap. "Oh, my gosh, y'all, that's Trina." From across the yard, her friend looked the same as she did a year ago. She still looked beautiful with a smile that went on for miles and her laugh shrill and full, easily carried across the yard. Everything seemed the same except her hair was a little longer than she wore it in college.

"Come on, y'all. You've gotta meet her."

"Trina!" Elizabeth called across the yard. Trina twirled and a squeal as high as a dog whistle came out of them both. Elizabeth let go of Jessica's arm, as Trina ran toward her, each girl quickly wrapping the other in an enormous hug and bouncing up and down.

Trina held Elizabeth at arm's length. "Girl, you look amazing! You're beautiful. Motherhood suits you." Trina smiled at the ring on Elizabeth's finger. "I'm still having a hard time believing you and Brady are actually engaged. Wow! You're one lucky girl." Trina gave him a side-long glance.

Elizabeth's heart took another hard leap as a familiar, yet long forgotten, pang of jealousy crept up from deep inside her gut. "I've gotta agree, I am the luckiest girl. It's still hard to believe he's all mine. After Grant was born, everything finally fell into place. God knows it took long enough."

Trina smiled again. "Well, I'm sure you'll both be great together. He's an amazing man." Trina raised her eyebrows and laughed a small laugh. Elizabeth's mouth gaped open. *Seriously, she's still hitting on Brady. Does the knowledge that we're engaged not show her he's off limits?* She turned away from Trina, putting some space between them.

Brady placed his arm around Elizabeth's waist, and she gave him a deep kiss on his lips.

Trina hip bumped Brady, knocking him off balance a little, causing him to break his kiss with Elizabeth. "I was just admiring Elizabeth's ring. I guess you're officially off the market. Congratulations!" She pulled him away from Elizabeth and wrapped her arms around him, a little lower than they needed to be. He returned the hug with a squeeze and a small smile on his face.

Elizabeth's stomach tied into knots. *He's not available anymore, Trina.* A vision of her tearing Trina's arm off Brady so hard it dislocated from its socket popped into her head.

Elizabeth smiled sweetly and pulled Brady next to her, holding him close. Her stomach knotted as she watched Trina with her future husband. *What made me invite her here? She hasn't grown up and is still acting like Brady's free for anyone to have. We might have shared in college, but we aren't sharing anymore.*

The tension in the air could be cut with a knife, and Brady, wanting to avoid any more strain between the two girls, pulled Elizabeth over to the fire pit to sit and relax. Their friends followed.

"So, Elizabeth, you and Trina were roommates. Since I just went to community college, what was it like when you first met?" Jessica asked.

"Yeah, all I know is that all three of you met at school and had a lot of fun." Chad raised his eyebrows and toasting the air with his beer.

Brady's face flushed. He glanced sideways at Trina, whose face wore a smirk, and slid closer to Elizabeth's side, grabbing her hand.

Elizabeth shook her head but started the story. "Well, we had lots of fun, even that first day. Trina and I hit it off right away. It was a little awkward walking into a room where a stranger already lived. She got there before me and had her things unpacked."

"Yeah, but I saved the best side of the room for you. Farthest from the door and you had the window." Trina flashed a smile.

"True." Elizabeth agreed. "Once my parents left, Trina helped me unpack and make my side of the room home. Then we went to the Freshman Roundup with some of the girls from our dorm."

Trina nodded and moved to the edge of her seat. "The Freshman Roundup was some competitions for freshmen to come together and get to know others. There was this three-legged race relay. We were a team."

Elizabeth felt herself relaxing as the memories flooded through her, and the knot that was growing in her stomach loosened. "Yeah, we were. A team that really sucked. Neither of us wanted to lose, and we had a hard time working together, and we found ourselves tripping all over the place." Elizabeth and Trina laughed.

"We were still on our way down the field to the first cone, and these two guys were coming toward us. They had already made the first turn. Trina made a comment, and I looked up."

Trina lifted a finger. "My comment, if I remember correctly, was, 'don't look now, but those hot guys are watching us and are a lot hotter up close.'"

Elizabeth raised her eyebrows. Yeah, they did! "So, of course, when told not to look, I looked. Then our feet got tangled, and we fell into the guys, and they fell on top of us. That's how we met Brady and his friend Trent." She and Trina laughed so hard tears flowed from their eyes.

"I guess you could say you fell head over heels for him." Jessica started to wipe the tears of laughter from her eyes as well.

"Yeah, literally." Elizabeth reached over to clasp Brady's hand and gave him a quick kiss on his lips. "Once we made sure no one was hurt, the guys decided it wasn't worth winning anymore. They helped us untie our ankles, and Brady helped me up from the ground. They were rushing a fraternity, and the Freshman Roundup was almost over, so they invited us to the fraternity house. Trina and I went and hung out there ever since, becoming college-long friends."

Trina's grin filled her face. "Yeah, we did. And we made some amazing memories."

Elizabeth glued a smile on her face as a sick feeling filled her heart.

It was quickly erased when Brady pulled her from her seat into his arms. "This woman took my breath away that first night—falling on top of me, and I have loved her in that position ever since."

Elizabeth rolled her eyes and pressed her palm against his cheek, glad to turn the discussion to her and Brady and away from her friendship with Trina. "I remember that night. Brady, you didn't let me out of your sight." She leaned in and brushed her lips against his.

"We danced, talked, and started making out under a tree in the backyard. I was just as lost in you as you seemed to be lost in me." He placed his hand on the side of her face so she couldn't look away. "We stayed together that night. Just talking. All night. We laid together, kissed, and talked. Not what I really wanted to do. She drove me wild, but something in me didn't want to mess it up. She didn't realize it, but she already had me." He placed another light kiss on her lips.

Elizabeth's heart fluttered. "How could I not have realized you wanted more than just being…"—she made air quotes with her finger. — "'friends with benefits.' You never said anything, and just agreed with me that we didn't have time for a relationship, that we didn't need a relationship." She leaned in for yet another kiss and became serious. "I was so blind." Maybe if she wouldn't have been so stubborn, she wouldn't be feeling like having Trina here was a bad idea.

"It doesn't matter. It all worked out." He smiled.

Jessica had a dreamy look spread across her face and she placed her hand on Chad's leg. "Hey, it's okay. He's here now. He loves you, and you two are awesome together. Some of us are just slower to the finish line than others. Look at me and Chad." Jessica tapped his thigh. "We knew each other for a long time, but I was stuck on his best friend. Which, of course, did not end well, and Chad was there for me. We finally started talking and hanging out more, and now here we are."

"Yeah, here we are. Like she said, some of us are slower getting to the finish line. It's just hard when your best friend's in the way." Chad engulfed Jessica in a deep kiss.

That's the truth, thought Elizabeth.

"So, Trina, is there anyone you left in Florida?" Debra piped in.

Trina looked around the group, her eyes lingering on Elizabeth and Brady. "No, I didn't leave anyone in Florida. There was a guy for a while this summer, but like all summer romances made at the beach, he had to get back to his job and his girl." Trina dropped her gaze and stared at the flames.

"You had a romance with a guy who was cheating on his girlfriend?" asked Deb, her eyes wide.

"Seriously?" Elizabeth was shocked that Trina just admitted to willingly being with a guy who had a girlfriend. Some things never change.

"Well, I sort of knew about this other girl, but didn't know his heart was with her at the time, and it seemed as if he thought there wasn't going to be any relationship. But as some things took shape, he realized there could be." Trina shrugged. "Finally, he came clean. He seems to have chosen her over me. For now, anyway." Her eyes fell and watched her fingers as they picked at the label on her beer bottle before quickly flicking over to Brady.

. Brady shifted in his seat and turned his head.

Chad glanced around the fire pit. His eyes made contact with Christian's, who raised his brows. "So, did anyone catch the score of the game today? Tennessee kicked some ass and looked awesome on the field," Chad commented.

He and Christian started talking about the game, rehashing the top plays. Soon the others joined in and the discussion was averted from Trina's drama to a topic worth talking about.

Chapter 9

The moon was high in the sky. It was getting late, and the party was dying down. The girls headed into the house to clean the kitchen and Brady, Chad, and Christian carried tables and chairs into the garage. "Place them right here. I'll put them away later." Brady directed and piled some extra cases of beer and drinks in the corner.

The kitchen door opened, and Trina came into the garage. "I just wanted to say bye before I left."

"It was nice to meet you, Trina." Chad waved and gave a small nod. Trina answered him with a quick wave of her hand and a small turn up of her lips.

"Bro, do you need anything else?" Christian asked.

"Not in here. If y'all could make sure all the trash is picked up outside, that'd be great." Brady tossed a black trash bag at his brother. Christian's eyes passed between Brady and Trina before he walked out of the garage.

Once Christian left, Trina walked to the door and closed it, then she sauntered slowly over to Brady. His eyes followed her yet tried not to watch her hips as they swayed. He tried to ignore the way his heart picked up a rhythm and betrayed him.

"It was great seeing you again. I'm glad I was invited." Her voice was soft and seductive, and she ran her fingers across his chin and laid her other hand on his chest.

Brady cleared his throat and sucked in his lower lip. "Elizabeth seemed happy to see you."

She pushed her gaze into his and held tight to his chin, keeping him from looking away. "Yeah, it was good seeing her. But better seeing you again." Her eyes wandered down to his lips, which parted slightly as if he was trying to breathe.

Brady again sucked in his lower lip and took a deep breath. He grabbed her hands. "Trina, what are you doing? I told you, I'm with Elizabeth."

She still held his brown eyes tightly with her blue. "Your words say one thing. Your body tells a different story."

His breathing hitched, and he stepped away, putting much-needed space between them as he tried to get control of his body's reaction. "Trina..."

She took a step and pressed her body against his and narrowed her eyes. "Brady." She whispered.

He swallowed hard and felt his body reacting to her. *Get it together, Brady. You can't go there again.* He pushed her away from him. She could not have this power over him. Elizabeth had his ring on her finger. Elizabeth held his heart. Elizabeth was right there in their kitchen.

She grabbed his face and forced him to look at her. "You didn't stop me this summer." Their gaze froze for a beat, and Brady felt an unwanted heat grow deep in his body.

Finally, he broke free from her and turned away. "I don't know what you think will happen here, but I love Elizabeth.

You need to go. You need to go now." He snapped at her. His heartbeat sped up, and heat crawled up his neck. He stood there, not moving, and didn't turn around until he heard her feet cross the garage, the door open and close, and a car start and pull away.

He dropped down hard on the lid of a cooler and placed his head in his hands. "What the hell was that, Brady?" He raked his hands through his hair, trying to compose himself. The garage door opened with a jerk, and he jumped to his feet.

Christian stood there watching him. "Again, are you good, bro?"

Brady shook his head as he pushed past Christian, heading out to the yard to help the guys clean up.

Elizabeth finished putting the last of the dishes in the dishwasher as Jessica and Debra put the leftovers away. Elizabeth dried her hands on a towel and caught a quiet look pass between the two girls as they worked. She crossed her arms across her chest. "What's up? Seems like y'all have something to say."

Jessica and Debra continued working, neither spoke up. Elizabeth glared at them and

Debra sighed. "Okay, first of all, I want to say I've known Brady a long time. I've heard your name come up in his conversations more than once over the years, even before last summer when he found out you were pregnant. Christian told me he had a thing for you when we were at y'all's college graduation.

So, I know what I'm gonna say is not an issue." Debra stopped and took a big breath as she gave Jessica a smug look.

Jessica rolled her eyes. "Whatever. Fine, I'll talk... So, Trina and you... shared everything, including Brady, at college, right?" Jessica looked intently at Elizabeth.

Elizabeth rolled her eyes toward the ceiling. "That was direct. But yes. Sex, was just sex."

Jessica grabbed Elizabeth's arms. "I'm sorry to bring all this bad baggage up, but I just get a bad feeling. Trina seems a little too close to Brady—if that makes sense. I mentioned it to Deb earlier." Debra opened her mouth to speak, but Jessica held up her hand so she could finish. "Look, I know he loves you, Elizabeth, and I don't doubt it, but it's her intentions I don't trust."

It wasn't just me picking up a weird vibe from Trina tonight. Elizabeth stopped fidgeting with the towel in her hands and laid it on the counter. "Was I stupid inviting her?" She looked at her friends, her brows lifted with concern before she continued. "I'm not usually the jealous type, but whenever she looked at Brady, I couldn't get out of my head that she was with him in college and had feelings for him. She was so competitive when it came to him. I sort of felt that again tonight."

"Look, I'm sure it's strange. I really don't know what to say except Brady loves you. He wouldn't do anything to jeopardize what you both have."

Elizabeth gave Debra a small smile. She knew what she said was true but just couldn't shake the uneasy feeling growing inside her.

"I think that inviting Trina here tonight was just a bit much. Are you okay with her being around Brady or him being around her?" Jessica leaned on the kitchen bar. "I know if Chad had a girl hanging all over him, I wouldn't be dealing with it as well as you are. He's my man, and girl's better keep their hands off. Especially if they have a history of sex together."

Debra brought a bottle of wine over and filled some fresh glasses. "I've got to agree. You are way too understanding."

Jessica took a sip of wine. "I'm concerned with how Brady hugged her, and she's been hanging on him. They seemed pretty chummy. Are you sure they haven't seen each other since college?"

Elizabeth searched the faces of her friends. "Really, y'all are so untrustworthy. I don't have anything to worry about. He hasn't talked to her since college, or he would have told me." She took a sip of her wine. "As for Trina, she's just that way. She's always been very touchy-feely. She knows there's nothing she can do to get between Brady and me anymore." Elizabeth tried her best to look more confident in her words than she felt. She swallowed at the hard knot in her stomach. "Anyway, even if I can't trust Trina, I have total trust in Brady. He won't do anything. He loves me, and his family is the most important thing to him."

Elizabeth put her wineglass on the counter and reached for a hand from each friend. "Thank you for being such caring friends. Anyway, Deb, I'm sure if there were any issues, Christian would let you know, and you'd tell me. So, it's all good."

Elizabeth gave her friends a large confident smile but didn't miss the fact that Deb turned away from her gaze.

"Deb? What?" She squeezed her hand and pulled her arm forward. "If you know something, tell me."

Deb stared into her wineglass. "Just talk to Brady. Let him know you're not happy with how close they were tonight."

Elizabeth let go of Jessica and Deb's hands and picked up her wineglass. "I will." She kept her eyes on her friends and took a big sip of wine. "I promise."

Chapter 10

On Monday morning, Elizabeth watched Brady pull out of the driveway on his way to work, a contented smile curving her lips. She leaned her head back on the door frame and closed her eyes. Her insides warmed as she remembered the details of their after-party celebration. Once everyone left Saturday night, she still had an uneasy feeling about the Trina situation. Part of her wanted to confront Brady, but instead, she spent the rest of the weekend making sure he had no excuses to look other places for happiness or satisfaction. Elizabeth took charge in the kitchen, on the couch, and in their bed. She ensured that he was exhausted and well-loved when she was done with him. Sunday, she took more time on her appearance, wore sexier clothes that showed off her cleavage and other parts of her body he enjoyed, and gave him plenty of what he wanted whenever possible—with no baby in the house, it wasn't hard; she simply loved on her man.

Closing the door behind her, she walked to their room and stopped in front of the mirror. She stood sideways and rubbed her hand across her stomach. It wasn't as flat and tight as it used to be, but it still looked good, and she was working on it. Pregnancy helped her in the boob area, and she had more cleavage than she used to. "Yep, Brady would be crazy to not be interested in this." She winked at her reflection, snatched her book off the table, and went to sit on the patio to enjoy the little bit of peace and quiet she had left before Grant returned from his grandma's.

Her mind kept wandering, and she found it difficult to focus on the book in her hands. Getting up, she walked toward the garden filled with blooming lilies, marigolds, and gerbera daisies. She started pruning and weeding, which always relaxed her. "I'm twenty-four, a mom, and living with my fiancé. This time last year, I'd never have thought I'd be here." She reached out and touched one of the gerbera daisies. The silkiness of the red petal in her fingers filled her with a sense of calm. "Grant's almost seven months old. It's time I went back to work and used my degree. Sitting around all day while everyone else works isn't what I saw myself doing. I'm sure my mom would love to be Grant's babysitter."

Elizabeth sighed deeply and wandered back into the house. She opened her laptop on the counter and searched the abyss of the world wide web for something which might make her feel important, for what she wasn't sure.

She found herself shopping, without purpose, on one of her favorite stores' websites. She found some cute outfits for Grant, and a new blouse, and a pair of shoes for her. Clicking buy, an idea suddenly occurred to her. Main Street Boutique, the shop she worked at before Grant, could profit from having an online store and social media presence. She was sure of it.

Butterflies danced in her stomach. She started to draft a plan to take to Barbara Stanzel, the owner.

With newfound energy and purpose, Elizabeth contacted Brady's mom, asking if she could watch Grant for a little longer, then she put everything she had into a marketing plan for the new online store and social media account for Main Street Boutique

Elizabeth strolled toward Main Street Boutique with her head held high and a bounce in her step. As she opened the door, the scent of fruit and flowers met her nose, and music played quietly overhead. Barbara Stanzel, the owner, stocked the store with something for everyone and used her unique ability to guarantee that all finds were one of a kind.

Barbara's face lit up when she made eye contact with Elizabeth. "Hi, Elizabeth. I'll be with you in a sec." She continued checking out the last customer, and once they left, she locked up and came to talk with Elizabeth.

Barbara walked with a long and confident stride for a petite five-foot-two woman, who was almost sixty years old. Her short, dark hair was cut in a cute style that framed her face and made her brown eyes pop. Elizabeth loved her former boss and hoped that she would like what Elizabeth came to show her.

Barbara grabbed Elizabeth in a tight squeeze. "Oh, my goodness, Elizabeth! It's so good to see you. What brings you by the store? And where is that adorable baby of yours?"

Elizabeth's breath was pressed out of her like she was caught in a vise, and a smile erupted over her face. "It's good to see you, too. I miss this place. It's been months since I've been in here." Elizabeth pulled away and held on to the older lady's arms. "Grant is great. Brady's mom is watching him for me. I wanted to talk with you about something."

Barbara's shoulders twitched. "Okay. Let's go into the office and get comfortable."

Elizabeth followed her into the back of the store. There was a large storage area, and through it was an office with a desk, a small refrigerator and microwave, and a round table with three chairs. Elizabeth and Barbara sat at the table.

The butterflies, which had earlier danced in her stomach with excitement, now fluttered nervously. Taking a deep breath, Elizabeth took out her computer and started her presentation. She showed her the beginnings of the website she created, explaining how she felt this could increase the store's bottom line, bring in new business, and give the store a fresh, updated new look.

Barbara became thoughtful as she perused the website, clicking through the pages and selecting products. "I'm amazed that you spent your private time thinking about this. I've been wondering what I could do to take the store to the next level, but I just don't have it in me to focus on anything." She nodded as a smile spread across her face. "This is great, and I'd love for you to get on this right away. If you can work it out with the baby, I'd love to have you here at least two days a week. I'd prefer three if possible. My days have been crazy lately." Barbara's head shook as she stared at the ceiling. "Filling the shoes of you and Jessica has been harder than I thought. You two were hard workers, trustworthy, and fun to have around. It's hard to find students who want to work. If you're here three days, you could help me run the store and prepare the website." Mrs. Stanzel watched Elizabeth for her reaction.

Elizabeth's body froze as her mouth popped open. *That was easier than I thought.* She rubbed her face in her hands, trying to wipe the shock off.

Barbara continued. "I know this is sudden. We can wait a week or two if that makes you feel better. That should give you time to find a sitter for Grant. Of course, we can wait a couple of months if you don't think this is something you can really get into now."

This is just what she needed, and her heart sped up. "No, no. That's why I brought this to you today. I just can't believe you're this willing to bring me back. I think I can set up some sitting arrangements with my mom. She only works part-time. I could let you know before Friday."

Barbara pumped her arm. "Yes. That's awesome. I'd love to have you back in these walls, and your marketing expertise will be an amazing help. I'm excited about what you can do for the store."

Elizabeth skipped across the parking lot and did pirouettes in her excitement. Her body felt as if it were floating on air. With a newfound purpose, she stopped at the grocery store to pick up the ingredients to make Brady a special meal, then called Joanna to tell her she was on her way home.

"I can't believe how impressed Mrs. Stanzel was. I can't wait to help bring new business to the store." She decided to start a social media account right away and work on a website. Her smile filled her heart. The thought of helping the boutique's sales was like she had climbed Mount Everest.

"I'm gonna make the Main Street Boutique an amazing shopping experience for everyone. It'll take time and focus, but I know I can do this." Elizabeth looked at her reflection in the rear-view mirror and beamed.

Chapter 11

Excitement bubbled over inside Elizabeth, and she was ready to explode by the time they were settled at the kitchen table to eat the roast beef and potatoes she had made. "Guess what happened to me today?"

"What?" Brady was texting and didn't look up.

She rolled her eyes and quickly snatched his phone from his hands.

"Hey!" He lunged forward, trying to regain control of his phone, but Elizabeth was quicker and placed it out of reach.

She laid her hand over his, keeping them from moving. "I was trying to talk to you, and you were ignoring me." She held his gaze. "I have something I want to tell you."

Brady sat back and let out a heavy breath. "You're right. I'm sorry. I'll listen." He placed his hand on the table, palm up, and lifted his brow. "After you give me back my phone."

Elizabeth's lips turned up in a smirk, and she plopped his phone in his palm. "There. Now. Guess what happened to me today."

She told him all about the research she had completed, the website she started for Main Street Boutique and the social media accounts she set up. "The website and social media presence will take the boutique to the next level. I'm going to catalog the product in the store. That'll help us to keep up with an online inventory. Then I'll write up online specials and discounts for those who follow our social media accounts. I really hope it increases the revenue. She asked me to start working three days a week. I'll be there for the front of the store when necessary, but mostly to keep inventory up to date on the website and to take care of the online orders." She paused and took a breath, her eyes shining. "Isn't that awesome!"

Brady was watching her with a blank expression while he bit his bottom lip. She laid her hand on his arm. "Look, I'm sure you're concerned about me working and taking care of Grant, but I already talked to our moms. My mom's going to watch Grant Monday and Wednesday, and on Friday's your mom said she'll come here. They're both excited to spend more time with him."

Brady sighed deeply and looked up at the ceiling. This stopped Elizabeth in the middle of her sentence. "What's wrong?"

He chewed slowly, his mouth full of roast and potatoes. Slowly, he placed his fork on his plate and his hand over hers. "Aren't you happy with your life? Am I not doing enough?"

"I'm sorry. I don't understand." She shook her head slowly. *Where did he get that from?*

Brady's face dropped. "You don't need to worry about money. I make enough for both of us. Can't you be happy just being a mom? Isn't that enough?"

His reaction shocked her. She touched his cheek, making

sure she had his attention. "Brady, yes. You and Grant are so important to me. This has nothing to do with either of you. It's me. I need something else to do with my time. I need to feel like my college degree isn't being wasted. If I wait too long, I won't have any experience and won't be able to get a decent job. This won't take much time away from here, away from you two. I promise. It's just three days a week."

Brady played with his fork while she was talking. "I just don't want you to work too hard and wear yourself out. There's nothing wrong with being a stay-at-home mom. Both our mothers were. I work hard, so you don't have to."

Her eyes searched his. She didn't realize he felt this way, that he expected her to be a stay-at-home mom. That never crossed her mind. "I just need to do something. Grant is my chief priority." Hurt crossed his face. "And you, of course." She smiled at him and brushed her hand through his hair.

His gaze bore into her. They were quiet for a bit. She wanted to give him time to process what she said and sort through his emotions. "You've always been independent and headstrong, Liz. That's one thing that caught my attention in college." He gave a deep sigh and shrugged. "Okay. I want you to be happy. Go for it."

She got up and slid into his lap, wrapping her arms around his shoulders. "Thank you." A gleam of joy shined in her eyes and she placed a kiss on his soft lips. "I love you, Brady Warren. It's going to be so awesome. Mrs. Stanzel is excited to see what can come of this. I am too. There're so many possibilities."

He laughed and gave her another deep kiss, then started

to clean the kitchen while Elizabeth took Grant and got him ready for bed.

Chapter 12

"Hi, Mom. We're here." Elizabeth entered the sunroom of her parent's house.

"Well, there's my little man." Charlotte bounced in with excitement. She planted a kiss on her daughter's head and snatched Grant from her arms. Elizabeth laughed as her mother hummed her favorite song and danced with Grant through the room and into the kitchen, spinning and twirling with him. His head fell back as he closed his eyes and laughed his cute little belly laugh.

"Okay, Mom. I don't mean to rush out, but it looks like it's gonna start raining. They're calling for storms later, and I really want to be home before it gets bad." She caught her boy mid-spin and gave him a kiss on his chubby cheek and her mom a hug. "I love you both. I won't be long. Just running by the pregnancy center, then the mall. I'll call you when I'm on my way home."

"Elizabeth! So glad to see you." Deloris Green, the director of the Crisis Pregnancy Center, greeted her as she walked through the door, wrapping her in a powerful hug.

Elizabeth smiled as she hugged the lady back. "Hi. Mrs. Green. How are things going today?"

Deloris walked toward the meeting room, with Elizabeth following. "It's been a wonderfully busy day. We've been inundated with donations, and need to get them sorted, and the phone has been ringing non-stop. I'm glad you'll be taking over today's group. I have a meeting in a bit."

"I'm excited but a little nervous. I've never done this by myself. There's always been someone else with me."

Deloris flashed her an encouraging smile. "You'll do great. You're an amazing role model, and I have total faith in you."

The women in her group today varied in age from forty and scared about starting again with a baby when her youngest is in high school, to twenty-two and still in college. Elizabeth enjoyed her time talking with the women and praying with them. She shared her story about unexpectedly becoming pregnant, how she had to face the past she wanted to run from, and how the center helped her realize she could be a wonderful mom.

As the last of the group left, Elizabeth cleaned up and was ready to head to the mall.

"Ms. Elizabeth?"

Before her stood the young girl, pretty brown hair, and frightened brown eyes. "Just Elizabeth, please. I'm not much older than you. Leila, right?"

Leila nodded. "I know you're heading out, but do you have a minute?"

Elizabeth pulled the full bag from the trash can and tied it shut. "Of course. What up?" She sat down again, hoping Leila would feel more comfortable.

Leila followed her lead and took a seat. "How did you decide you could do this? Be a mom? Did you have your parents' support?"

"I did. It was my parents who believed in me more than I believed in myself. When I came here for the first time, and Deloris was talking to me about the choices I had, I was still confused. If it wasn't for the help of my parents, I'm not sure I would've kept my baby." A pang of sadness passed through Elizabeth's heart at the realization of the truth in that statement. She looked at Leila. There was fear in her eyes. Elizabeth's heart went out to her as she took her hand. "What's wrong? What can I help you with?"

Tears filled Leila's eyes. "My mom and I have never had a great relationship. When my parents got divorced, she blamed me. I dated anyone she didn't want me to, and this is the product of me making my mom mad."

Leila paused and wiped at the stray tear that ran down her cheek. "Anyway, to make a long story short, she kicked me out of her house. She said I'm twenty-two and should be on my own. That's why I'm here. I used the little money I had, purchased an airline ticket from Florida, and moved in with my dad and stepmom. I just don't want to feel like a burden to them, and I need a job, but who would hire me?" She stopped her rambling and took a deep breath.

"What kind of job are you looking for?"

Laila's eyes went wide. "Well, I only have experience in retail. I've worked with customers and worked on registers."

Elizabeth leaned forward, forcing Leila to look at her. "I've lived in this town my entire life. We have a lot of small businesses that are always looking for people to work. I know a lot of the owners. I'll ask around and help you find a job."

A small smile spread across Leila's face. Elizabeth passed her a box of tissues as the girl sniffled. She took a tissue and wiped her eyes and nose. "Thank you so much, Elizabeth. I appreciate it."

Elizabeth waved off her gratefulness. "Not a problem at all. What I want from you in the meantime is to go home and have a talk with your dad and stepmom. It sounds like your dad's a great guy. I'll call you in a couple of days about that job."

Elizabeth stood up and gave her a hug and left the pregnancy center for the day.

Elizabeth enjoyed her alone time shopping, and as she exited the mall, the rain started to fall. "Well, here it goes." Elizabeth wrapped herself in her windbreaker, putting up the hood to cover her hair, and tore across the parking lot with her head down against the raindrops. She unlocked her car and threw the bags with her purchases in the back seat, slammed the door quickly, and jumped into the front right before the drizzle became a downpour.

She let out a big breath, buckled her seat belt, and placed

both hands on the wheel. Elizabeth watched a lady running across the sea of concrete with her little boy in tow. The rain, falling harder now, plastered her hair against her head as she tried to move her son along, but he stomped in every puddle he could find, soaking himself from head to foot. "That was close. A minute later, I'd look like them. I'm glad I left Grant with Grandma."

As Elizabeth pulled out of the mall parking lot, the rain made it difficult to see the road ahead. Cautiously she merged onto the interstate toward home as her wipers, now at full speed, couldn't keep up with the water spilling from the sky. The rain quickly became a torrential downpour. The sound of the rain pelting the roof drowned out the music coming from the car's speakers.

Slowing her speed, Elizabeth put on her hazard lights and crawled down the interstate, staying a safe distance from the other cars as the rain started to pond on the road. She put her turn signal on and slightly turned the wheel. Suddenly she felt the tires of her car slide on the slick road. She tried to turn into the slide, but the car lifted from the road as the wheels left the concrete. It started sliding of its own accord.

She was no longer in control of her car. Her breathing quickened. Her pulse raced. She rocketed toward the concrete barrier, which protected her from colliding with the oncoming traffic.

Elizabeth's mind flashed to Grant and Brady. Fear enveloped her as the thought that she might never hold either of them again came to her mind. She braced for impact and hoped that no other cars were sliding toward her.

An overwhelming need embraced her, to remain calm and to relax.

She closed her eyes and took a deep breath, right before she crashed into the concrete barrier. A sound like a gun going off met her ears. She was punched in the face by her airbag. The car spun away from the barrier and rammed into another. It wasn't over. Like a ball in a pinball machine, the car spun into another car, and slid unnaturally to the other side of the lane making another hard impact with something else.

Chapter 13

Elizabeth was barely able to open her eyes. She noticed red flashing lights, and a piercing sound filled the air. Something blocked most of her sight, and her body couldn't move. Her pulse quickened, and her breath came in quick gasps as fear embraced her.

"Miss, please be still and relax. You were in a car accident, and you're in an ambulance. We're taking you to County Hospital. You'll be okay."

Elizabeth's eyes worked hard to focus.

"Can you tell us your name?"

Elizabeth fought through the fog that covered her brain. Her hand closed on an oxygen mask over her mouth, which was why her vision seemed blocked at first. She reached up to take it off. She closed her eyes and tried hard to focus on the question. "I'm Elizabeth." Her voice was almost inaudible.

"Good. Elizabeth, you were unconscious when we got to the wreck. Does anything hurt?"

Elizabeth again struggled to think of an answer to this man's question but completed a quick mental inventory of her body. "No. I feel fine... I think. I was on my way home from the mall. I need to call my mom. She has Grant. Brady, he needs to know.

My parents need to know. They'll all be worried." Her eyes became wide, and she wiggled her body, trying to break free from whatever was keeping her still.

"Elizabeth, relax, please. We found your phone and called your mom. She was listed as an emergency contact. She and your dad are meeting us at the hospital." The paramedic put pressure on her shoulders and attached the oxygen mask over her face again.

Her breathing calmed, and her eyes closed, drifting off.

The commotion of the Emergency Room floated into Elizabeth's consciousness. She found herself alone in a room attached to machines. She tried to move her head to see her surroundings but found she was limited in neck movement. She brought her hand to her neck and felt a brace. Feeling panic rise in her chest, Elizabeth tried to sit up, but her head swam with pain.

The door opened and her parents rushed through, followed by a man in a long white coat. Seeing her daughter awake, Charlotte wrapped Elizabeth in a gentle yet desperate hug. Elizabeth did her best to hug her mom back, but with all the chords hanging from her, it was difficult.

"Mom, I'm so sorry. I don't really know what happened. Where's Grant? Did anyone call Brady?" Her hands pushed on the pain that pounded on the sides of her head.

"Elizabeth," the doctor interrupted. "Our first concern was

making sure you were stable. You'll be heading soon for an MRI to make sure there aren't any internal injuries. You hit your head hard and were unconscious for a bit." He clicked buttons on the pad he had in his hands. "Does anything else hurt? Your legs, arms?"

Elizabeth continued to massage her temples. "No. I feel fine, just my head feels like someone's banging it with a hammer, and I feel nauseous if I move."

He nodded. "Those are both normal symptoms with a head injury. We are taking care of them, and hopefully, those symptoms will feel better soon." He typed some notes, then, being positive and upbeat, excused himself and left the family alone. Charlotte sat down in a chair close by while her dad leaned against the wall of the room, texting.

"I couldn't get a hold of Brady on the phone, so I left a message on his voicemail and just sent him a text." He looked lovingly at his daughter.

Elizabeth closed her eyes. The lights made her head hurt. "Mom and Dad, you never answered me. Where's Grant?"

Charlotte squeezed Elizabeth's hand. "He's with Jacob and Stacey. When I got the call, you were in the hospital; I rushed to their house. Jacob had just pulled in. His timing was perfect. He said he'd be glad to watch Grant for me."

Grant's with Jacob! Can he even take care of a baby?

Charlotte read Elizabeth's thoughts. "It's okay. He knows how to take care of babies. I've seen him in the nursery at church. Relax. Anyway, Stacey will be home soon to help him, and Kristen's there."

"Kristen?" Elizabeth laughed. "I'm sure she'll be a big help." Elizabeth rolled her eyes and tried to sit up, but the tubes kept her from being able to move, and her head started to spin. She laid back down and her hands went up to the brace around her neck. "What's up with this thing?" She tried to get it off.

"Elizabeth, enough! That's just a precaution. Once you have your MRI, it can come off. It will only be for a little while. You need to be still." Jackson sat on the other side of her bed and squeezed her hand.

She looked into her father's eyes, and her breathing calmed. "Dad, the accident. Did anyone else get hurt? How's my car?"

Jackson smiled. "No one else was injured. There was only one other car involved, and that car was fine. Miraculously, you didn't hit anyone else. I don't know how." He brushed some hair off of Elizabeth's face. "Your car is another story. We'll need to find you a new one."

Before Elizabeth could think through what she was told, a nurse came to get her to take her for an MRI. After what seemed like days but was really only a little more than an hour, Elizabeth was back in her room and placed back in her bed. Brady still hadn't arrived.

"Have you heard back from Brady yet, Dad?" Elizabeth asked once she was comfortable again.

"No, not yet."

"Can I have my phone, and I'll call Christian? See if he can find him."

Charlotte gave her the phone.

Elizabeth dialed Christian. He answered on the first ring.

Unfortunately, Brady was on a jobsite and couldn't get to his phone, but Christian said he'd contact the site and get a message to Brady right away.

She hung up and relayed the message to her parents. A feeling of unease mixed with the pain in her head and the nauseousness of her stomach. She had lied to her parents. Christian didn't know where Brady was. He hadn't heard from him all day, but he was going to look for him now.

Exhaustion overtook her, and Elizabeth found it impossible to keep her eyes open.

When she woke up, she wasn't sure what time it was, but a doctor was in the room. He informed them that her concussion was not serious. He was going to prescribe some medication to help her with the pain, and she needed to rest. Her brain needed a break.

She was released from the hospital soon after and settled into the back seat of her parent's car. Looking out the window and watching the rain that still fell, she couldn't help but wonder where Brady was and why he didn't answer all the calls and messages. The uneasy feeling returned, and she couldn't ignore the queasy feeling starting to make its way up from her stomach to her throat.

"Dad, pull over, quick!"

Her dad pulled to the side of the road with just enough time for Elizabeth to open her door and puke.

She was relaxing in her favorite spot, the couch in the sunroom, when Jacob walked in holding Grant with Stacey not far behind. Grant let out a squeal which sent a pinprick of pain shooting through Elizabeth's skull but filled her heart with love at the same time. She winced.

Charlotte took Grant from Jacob and eased down gently next to her daughter. Elizabeth embraced her son. They rested their foreheads against each other, and Elizabeth inhaled her baby's scent. "Thanks so much for watching him."

Jacob sat on the chair across from her. "No problem. He was great."

Charlotte reached over and took Grant from Elizabeth. "You know what? Why don't I give this cutie a bath and keep him here tonight? You don't need to worry about him crying, and your head needs a rest. When Brady gets here, you two can go on home and take care of you. I'll bring him over in the morning."

That was just what she needed, a quiet night's rest. Her mom was the absolute best. "That would be great, Mom. But are you sure?"

Jackson breezed into the room and swept the baby into his arms. "It's late already. We're going to get him ready for bed. Say good night to Mommy, Grant." He blew raspberries as she stole a kiss and waved at him as her parents took him up to his room.

"Do you need anything? A cup of tea or coffee?" Stacey asked.

"Tea would be great. Thanks, Stace."

Elizabeth leaned her head back and let out a sigh. Her head still pounded with a dull thud, causing her stomach to churn. She closed her eyes, wishing that she had Brady's shoulder to lean on and that he was holding her, comforting her.

She turned her attention toward Jacob. "Thank you for watching Grant. I really appreciate it." He was a lifesaver.

"Don't thank me. I did what any friend would do. How are you feeling?"

"I've got a concussion, but I'll take it. It could have been so much worse. That was scary. I thought I was—" A sob burst out of her, and she brought her hands to her face. The fear of never seeing her baby again engulfed her, and Brady not being there to console her was too much to bear.

Jacob wrapped his arms around her. "Hey, it's alright. Nothing bad happened." He gave her a reassuring squeeze and rubbed her back.

With her head resting comfortably on his chest. He just held her until the tears and crying stopped and her breathing relaxed.

"Here's your tea, Liz." Stacey sat down on the couch as Elizabeth pulled herself away from Jacob, wiped her face, and reached for the mug of hot tea.

Breathing in the cinnamon and orange aroma emanating from her mug calmed Elizabeth further. "Thanks, Stacey."

"Umm, Elizabeth…" Her heart jumped as Brady entered the

room.

Jacob got out of the way so Brady could take his rightful place by her side. Brady gave him a half smile and wrapped Elizabeth up in his arms.

Stacey threw him an irritated glance. "Well, you finally made it."

"Yeah, I know. I'm sorry it took me so long." Brady cupped Elizabeth's face in his hands, searching her eyes. "Are you okay? I can't believe I couldn't get there. I am so sorry. Are you sure you're okay?"

Elizabeth cuddled tightly into his side as he wrapped his arms around her and hid his face in her hair. She wanted to know where he was, to hear his excuse why he wasn't there when she needed him most, but for now, she was exhausted, her head hurt, and she was just glad he was there. "I'm good. I'm just tired. Mom and Dad are gonna watch Grant for us tonight. Just take me home. I want to go to sleep in my bed."

He looked at her and kissed her. "I'll go tell my little man goodnight and let your parents know we're leaving."

Elizabeth watched Brady leave, then turned to Stacey and Jacob. "Thank you both. I really appreciate it."

Stacey leaned in and gave her a gentle hug. "You're welcome. Let me know if you need anything. Okay? I'll call you in the morning."

Then Jacob came over to her. She reached up, grasping his hand. "Jacob, seriously. Thank you. I am sure you watching my son wasn't fun for Kristen."

"Oh, whatever. She went to the room to watch TV. Stacey

and I had a good time with the little guy. He was a lot of fun. Anyway, I'm glad you're good. I really am." He gave her a hug.

"Tell Kristen I said thank you, please."

He laughed and nodded as he turned to walk out and shook hands with Brady.

Brady sat next to her, wrapping his arm around her shoulder. "So, are you ready? Your mom explained to me your medications and things to watch out for." Brady stared at the wall for a minute, then turned to look in Elizabeth's eyes. "Your parents aren't happy with me."

Elizabeth sighed. "I'm not happy with you either, Brady. But I'm too tired to worry about it now. You can explain things in the morning. I want to go home."

Chapter 14

Lying in bed, with Elizabeth's head on his shoulder, Brady held her in his arms, wanting to never let go. He closed his eyes tight. *What were you thinking, Brady? You almost lost the love of your life tonight. You weren't there for her, and for what reason?*

Brady opened his eyes and wiped the hair from her face. "I love you, Elizabeth." He whispered. "I promise to never hurt you again. I'll always be here for you when you need me." He brushed a gentle kiss on her forehead.

Brady reached out for Elizabeth and rolled over in bed. His eyes flew open as his hand hit an emptiness on the mattress. He sat up and placed his face in his hands, trying to control his breathing and clear his head. Brady had a hard time falling asleep last night because he was scared to take his eyes off her. Finally, falling into a sleep filled with nightmares, he tossed and turned, fighting the demons that stirred in the night.

In his nightmare, Elizabeth disappeared. He ran across campus. It reminded him of their college, but he couldn't be sure. He looked everywhere for her but couldn't find her. He and Grant were alone on the campus or in the world. It seemed to be his fault, but it wasn't clear as to why she was gone. When he looked up, Trina had her arms out to him, a menacing laugh coming from deep within her.

Even as he sat on his bed and his breathing became regular, he couldn't clear pictures from his mind, or the empty feeling in his chest. It continued even after he got out of bed and threw water on his face.

Trudging slowly downstairs, he found Elizabeth in the kitchen, drinking coffee, and eating a cinnamon raisin bagel. He stood staring at her. What he saw stopped his heart. The left side of her face was covered in a purple and red bruise, and with the shorts she had on, he could see that her knee looked swollen; It would end up with an ugly bruise as well.

He sat down next to her, engulfing her in a hug. Tears fell down his face. He almost lost her. The girl who is a part of all his favorite memories was almost taken from him. His heart felt empty, and he rested his chin on her head.

"Elizabeth, I am so, so sorry I wasn't there for you yesterday. It should have been me who met you at the hospital and brought you home." He hugged her and kissed the top of her head. She hugged him back stiffly.

Irritation and disappointment filled her eyes and lined her mouth. Sadness shrouded her face. "Where were you, Brady? I talked to Christian. He didn't know where you were, either. I lied to my parents and told them he said you were on a job site. I could tell that he was surprised you weren't answering your cell. What the hell! I was unconscious in an ambulance, and the man I love couldn't be found. What the hell, Brady!" Her eyes caught his and grabbed hold.

The look she shot at him was filled with daggers. Hot daggers, and he felt the heat. He knew he screwed up, but the reality of how bad was there in her eyes. He hurt her, not just physically, but in her heart.

"I'm sorry. I was at a work site and left my phone in my truck. I had turned it off because of a meeting I'd been in earlier. I didn't hear it and forgot to check it. By the time I got back to the office, it was late. Everyone had gone home. I went to my office to complete some paperwork. I wasn't in a hurry to get home because I knew you were having a day for yourself and then dinner with your parents, and I…"

He paused and raked his hands through his hair as he searched her face. The hair that was always hanging out of place was there again, and he tucked it carefully behind her ear. "… I got caught up with something…" His voice hitched in his throat, and he moved his gaze toward the window for a second before peering back at her. "… Then Christian came by when he checked the security cameras with his phone app and noticed my truck. He told me about the accident and that you and your parents were trying to get a hold of me. That's when I realized my phone had been turned off all day."

That lock of hair fell in her face again, and he brushed it away, lifted her chin so he could see her eyes better. "I promise. And I can't tell you how sorry I am." He leaned in and kissed her. Her lips were cold and emotionless. He brought both his hands to her face. She tried to pull her eyes from him, but he held her tight. "Elizabeth, you should be angry. I know it. I would be. I messed up—big time! I will make it up to you, if at all possible. I promise."

His need to be near her and feel her lips on him was tremendous. His need for her to forgive him ate him alive. He leaned in and placed his lips on hers. They begged and pleaded for forgiveness. He found her finally returning his kiss and deepening it to show him he was forgiven.

"Now." He leaned back from her. "Today you're doing nothing. I'm going to take care of you and Grant. I called in to work, and of course they don't expect me today. Be prepared to get tons of help tomorrow. Today, though, all you have is me." Again, he gave her a kiss and helped her to the couch.

Chapter 15

The day was long. With nothing to do but lie around, read, and nap, Elizabeth quickly grew bored. Her head hurt too much to work on the website for the boutique, so she was trying to come up with ideas and write them down on notebook paper. With her head pounding and eyes aching, she threw her pad and pen on the table in front of her and laid her head on the soft cushion of the couch and stared up at the ceiling. Brady entered with some ibuprofen and a cup of hot tea.

"Hey, it's time for you to take these, and you need to give your brain a break anyway." He placed her tea on the table, handed her the pills and a glass of water. He sat next to her and laid her feet on his lap.

Elizabeth sighed and closed her eyes as Brady started to massage her feet, releasing the tension from her body. She felt herself melting into the couch. "Thanks, Brady. That feels amazing."

"You're welcome. Jessica just called to check on you and was wondering if you were up for a little company. She and Chad want to come over. She said they'd stop and grab some sandwiches if you're up to it."

Elizabeth met his gaze with a small smile. "That sounds great. Tell them I'd like that."

"Good, I will. Now why don't you take a nap? I'll wake you right before they show up." Brady leaned over and placed a kiss on her cheek, covered her with her favorite throw blanket, and gently caressed her cheek before leaving her on the couch.

Hushed voices talking in the kitchen woke her from her nap. Elizabeth stretched the sleep from her sore muscles and pried herself off the couch, her swollen knee making it a little difficult to walk. She smiled when she saw Jessica and Chad standing around the kitchen counter. She reached over, turning off the light to take the glare from the room.

Jessica gently wrapped her best friend in a comforting hug. "How are you? I was so worried." Jessica set Elizabeth free as Chad repeated the same gentle hug.

"That's true," he said. "She's been driving her poor grandmother and me crazy with worry. She would have been over here last night if I hadn't tied her to the bed." Chad, seeing Jessica's wide eyes, corrected himself.

"Oh, I'm sorry. I forgot that's not why I tied you to the bed." He raised his eyebrows at his girlfriend and blew her a kiss.

Elizabeth laughed, then grabbed her head. "Don't make me laugh. It hurts." She placed a hand over her forehead as a grimace covered her face. Brady quickly wrapped her in a hug.

"You, okay?" He said with guilty concern.

"Brady, don't. It's fine." Elizabeth wiggled out of his embrace as irritation gripped her heart. She threw the refrigerator door open and got the pitcher of sweet tea out and poured herself a glass. She took her pills, downing the entire glass of tea as Chad and Jessica looked on.

"Now that you're awake, are you ready to eat?" Brady opened the sandwiches Chad and Jessica brought with them, and they all sat at the table.

Elizabeth's mouth watered. "Wow, this smells amazing! Thanks, y'all. I didn't realize how hungry I was. I'm glad Brady told you two to come over." She leaned over and gave Brady a kiss before she remembered she was still mad at him. She pulled back quickly and turned to her food.

After dinner was finished, they all helped clean up, and the guys went outside. Elizabeth, feeling tired, led Jessica to the couch to rest.

"Okay, so what's going on? You can't hide the tension between you and Brady. You keep giving him the cold shoulder. Why?" Jessica settled next to her on the couch.

Elizabeth sighed and told Jessica about how Brady was nowhere to be found Saturday. Even Christian didn't know where he was. "It bothers me. I feel like there's something going on. Something he's not telling me. I feel it in my gut." Tears pricked at the corners of her eyes.

Jessica reached for Elizabeth's hand. "Aww, honey. It's all fine. He's a man, after all, and losing track of time and being irresponsible is part of their DNA. I know there's nothing to be worried about." She hugged Elizabeth.

Elizabeth tried to feel comforted by Jessica's words, but she couldn't shake the doubt that filled her.

After Chad and Jessica left, Elizabeth was getting ready for bed when Brady came in and started a bath and added some of her favorite essential oils.

As the tub was filling, he turned toward her and wrapped her in a hug. Elizabeth felt her heart miss a beat at his touch, yet she was still angry. Breaking away from him, she cleared her throat before she could speak. "What's going on?" She looked deep into his eyes, trying to dig out what she felt was hidden in their depths.

Brady moved his hand to her the bottom of her shirt. "I want you to relax, and a nice hot bath is the perfect way."

She placed her hands over his, stopping them from lifting her shirt. "I feel like there's something you're not telling me. What is it?"

He shook his head. "I just feel bad. I almost lost you, and I wasn't there." He brushed his hand across her cheek, resting it there, and softly lifted her face to meet his. His lips brushed hers. "You're everything to me, Elizabeth, and I put something before you. Telling you I'm sorry is just not enough." His mouth covered hers. Desperate. Elizabeth's heart leaped in her chest. It took her a second to get her heartbeat back to its regular rhythm and her breathing in check.

He gently pulled her shirt up and off her body. This time she let him. "This night is all about you." Looking down, his eyes became hungry as he reached around, unhooked her bra, and removed it, releasing her breasts.

Elizabeth's breath grew shallow as Brady's hands slowly slipped down her side to push her shorts gently down her legs. She stood in front of Brady, the only one naked in the room. She stepped closer to him. A desire deep inside her pushed her forward, and Elizabeth devoured him with her eyes.

Brady returned her gaze and held her hands in his. "You're taking a bath. You need to soak your sore muscles and your knee." Brady's voice came out husky, and he helped her into the tub. "Now, relax. I'll be waiting for you, but no hurry."

The water was hot but not burning, and she melted into the back of the tub and closed her eyes. The hot water felt good on her aching knee, and she felt the stress of her muscles melt away.

Elizabeth was drying herself off when suddenly Brady appeared in the bathroom and whisked her off her feet and laid her gently on the bed.

"Brady," she squealed. Her heart stopped when she saw the look in his eyes as he towered over her, staring at her naked body. He pressed his lips gently to hers and crawled onto the bed. He broke their kiss and brushed his hand across her face.

"Brady?" Elizabeth let the question in his name hang in the air between them.

He shook his head slowly as a tear trailed down his face. "I was stupid. I promise it won't happen again. I should've been there for you, and I wasn't. It should've been me with you in the hospital. I'm so sorry, I screwed up."

Elizabeth's heart finally gave in and opened back up to him.

She placed her hands on his face and searched his eyes. "I'm okay, and you're here now. Continue proving to me how sorry you are and maybe you'll be forgiven. Right now, I'm going to bed." She sent him a wicked smirk and placed a quick peck on his lips, rolled over, and fell asleep.

Chapter 16

Elizabeth's week was relaxing and filled with help. Her mom and Joanna stayed with her during the day, and Brady hovered around her at night. By the end of the week, boredom took hold, and she thought she might go stir crazy if she didn't get out. Joanna took Grant to her house on Friday morning, so Elizabeth could spend some quiet time by herself.

Her head felt better than it had all week, so she decided the boutique would give her the change she desired. She hopped in the surprise car she received from Brady and drove the couple of blocks to the boutique. The car was brand new, with all the bells and whistles anyone could ever need. Elizabeth was sure it was a gift to buy her forgiveness, and it worked a little, but he still wasn't one hundred percent forgiven.

Her phone rang as she pulled into the boutique's parking lot. "Shoot. Hello?" nothing. "How do I answer my phone on this thing... oh. Here... Hello?" Elizabeth was breathless by the time she answered the phone.

"Dang, girl. What's wrong with you? It sounds like I interrupted something."

Trina.

That familiar bang of jealousy—or maybe it was

dread—filled her stomach. "Hey, Trina. What's up?" "Nothing much. Just calling to check on you. I heard about your accident. Are you okay?"

"Yeah, I'm doing better, thanks. How'd you hear about my accident?" Elizabeth racked her brain to remember if anyone she knew had Trina's number. Only one person came to mind.

"Brady called me and told me. He was so worried. I guess he wasn't around when it happened. You couldn't find him?"

Elizabeth's stomach churned. Trina always seemed to pop up, yet shouldn't she have been heading back to Florida soon? "Yeah, that's right, but everything's getting back to normal."

"Well, that's good to know. Do you need anything? I'll come by and help if you want me to, or if you don't need anything, maybe we can go out to eat. Have a little girl's night."

Elizabeth took a deep breath. She and Trina. They were best friends just a year ago, even though things between them were always a contest when it came to guys—Brady included. She had to know the contest was over. Right? He belonged to Elizabeth. "You know what, how about dinner tonight? Come to my house, and we'll go somewhere. I'm sure you're leaving soon to go back to Florida."

Elizabeth thought she heard a sigh come through the phone. "Yes, I am, and I'd love to see you before I go. I'll come by tonight."

Brady got off work early and was busy digging holes and planting some rose bushes in the front of their house to surprise Elizabeth before she got home. She had been wanting some color in the front for a while, so he was making sure it happened. It was hard work. The day was hot, and the humidity was so thick you could cut it with a knife. He lost his shirt a while ago, and sweat glistened on his chest while dirt stuck to his damp skin. He wore a bandana around his head to keep the sweat from dripping in his eyes.

"Hey, Brady!"

He jumped at the interruption, prickling his finger on one of the thick thorns of the rose bush he had just finished planting. "Shit!" His finger flew to his mouth to suck the drop of blood that appeared.

As he turned, he noticed toes, which were well kept and painted in a rose pink and tucked into gold sandals. His eyes moved up the long legs, sexy and tanned, covered in not much of a pair of shorts. He continued to travel his gaze upward to the tight sleeveless shirt which clung right below the breasts. exposing the tight, shapely belly and bellybutton piercing which adorned it.

When their gaze finally met, Brady was looking into Trina's blue eyes. A smile mixed with uncertainty clouded his face. He haphazardly wiped his hands on his jeans.

"Hey, Trina. What brings you by?" He eyed her warily. Why

was she here? She doesn't take hints very well that she isn't wanted around.

"Oh, nothing. Elizabeth and I were planning on getting together tonight. I'm heading back to Florida soon, so we're gonna have a girls' night."

Her eyes roved over his entire body. His jeans were dirty, his torso was sweaty and shirtless, and his face was unshaven. "Looks like I got here just in time. You've been working hard and could probably use a drink. Should I go inside and grab you something?"

Brady stared at the girl in his yard and stumbled over his words. "Sure. Water'd be great."

Trina threw him a side grin and walked up the steps into the house, shaking her hips a little more than necessary. Brady followed close behind, trying hard to keep his eyes off those hips and on the ground in front of him.

As soon as they entered the house, Brady headed for the sink to wash the dirt from his hands as Trina filled a glass with water and cut up a lime that was sitting on the counter. She placed a slice of lime in the glass and handed him the drink. "Here, just like you like it—room temp with a lime."

Brady took the water and watched her as she pulled out an ice-cold Corona from the refrigerator, popped the top, and pushed a lime wedge inside. She leaned on the counter next to him as he took a sip of his lime-flavored water.

"So, what really brings you by? I didn't realize you and my fiancé had much to talk about. You haven't talked with her since our party, have you?" Brady emphasized the word fiancé as if to remind her that he and Elizabeth had moved on from their college years.

"Well, I was worried about her after the accident and called to check on her, and you, to see if there was anything you needed." Trina sauntered over to Brady and cornered him against the counter.

Trina ran her fingers across his chin and laid her hand on his chest. She fixed her gaze on him, keeping him from looking away. A smirk crossed her face, and she brushed her lips against his.

His eyes popped wide as he stepped to the side, trying to put as much space as possible between himself and another bad decision. "Trina...what the hell!" He took some slow deep breaths trying to control the heat rising in his groin.

She grabbed his face making him look at her. They held each other's gaze, and Brady felt the familiar, yet unwanted heat grow deeper throughout his body, causing a throbbing which was becoming harder to ignore.

The sound of footsteps at the front entrance snapped him back to reality. Brady stepped away from Trina. He took a big gulp of water and stared out the window, trying to calm his breathing. He closed his eyes, willing his blood to settle. When Elizabeth walked into the room, he turned, fully composed, and walked toward her with a smile on his face.

"Hey there, beautiful." He grabbed her in a hug and gave her a quick kiss, reminding his body and his heart that she was the one he wanted. She was the one he loved.

"Hi there, you." She answered him. "Trina, you're here early.

How long have you been here?"

"She just got here." He broke away from her, holding her gaze for just a second before turning to watch his son in his infant car seat slumbering peacefully. "How's our boy?" He took the infant seat from Elizabeth and carried it into the living room. Then he carefully unbelted Grant from its security and took him out to snuggle with him.

Chapter 17

Elizabeth's smile reached her eyes as she watched Brady cuddle with Grant. He was so gentle and sweet with him—the best dad ever. She turned to Trina and gestured toward the living room and took a seat on the couch next to Brady. "You never told me how you like Florida, Trina. I'm sure you're anxious to get back."

Trina made herself comfortable in the chair. "Yeah, I'm really loving it, except for being so far away from my parents, but Dad seems to be getting better. Anyway, it's everything we thought it would be when we talked about moving there."

A pang of envy hit Elizabeth in the gut. When she and Trina were in college, they always talked of moving to Florida after graduation to get away and start their adult lives on their own. "And there's never a lack of things to do, parties, guys, fun. Too bad you had to go and get responsible on me. We would really have had fun down there together."

"Yeah, well, sometimes life puts us on a different journey." Elizabeth hooked her arm around Brady, running her fingers through his hair and as she watched Grant sleep. "Tell me about your place. What's it like? Is it far from the water?"

Trina glanced at Brady. "Brady didn't tell you? He was there last summer." His eyes shot up momentarily toward hers before they turned back to watch Grant.

"He was at your place last summer?" Elizabeth looked at him, her eyes a shroud of confusion. "I knew he took a vacation to the beach last summer, but Brady, you never told me you saw Trina."

"No, silly." Trina shook her head. "He didn't just see me. I invited him down. He visited with Trent. They stayed at my place for the weekend." Trina sneered at the shock on Elizabeth's face. "Remember when I asked you if it would be okay if I asked him out? Well, I did. We had a good time." She paused and smirked at him. "Didn't we, Brady?"

Brady got up from the couch as the baby started to fuss. He paced the room, bouncing Grant to calm him. Elizabeth's eyes narrowed, glistening with tears. Trina seemed so pleased with herself for revealing this little secret. Elizabeth felt a sword of betrayal push deep in her heart. She hoped that the hurt Brady saw on her face tore a wound through him also.

"Did you go to Florida to see Trina last summer?" Elizabeth asked, her voice cracking.

Brady plopped down on the couch beside Elizabeth. "Yes, I went down when she asked me. Trent and I stayed with her. We weren't a thing, Elizabeth, you and me. We hadn't even talked since graduation. I remember thinking you might be there, too. I knew you both always talked about moving to Florida together after graduation. Maybe I was hoping. Anyway, it doesn't matter. Yes, I went." He paused, taking a second to search Elizabeth's eyes, trying to define the look she shot toward him. Finally, he let out a deep breath and lowered his head. Elizabeth's stomach started flopping and churning the small amount of food she had in it. She didn't like where this was going. What else happened last summer?

"To answer the question I know you're wondering, yes, we slept together."

Elizabeth couldn't stop the tears that rolled down her face. Last summer, she spent her time fearing what it would be like to be a mother. Wondering if she was ready to take on the responsibility. She had to change her dreams. Dreams of landing a job for a large company and traveling. There was no more doing things for herself. She no longer had the freedom to go wherever she wanted to go or do what she wanted to do, like move with her friend to Florida. She even walked away from Jacob and the relationship they started. All because she was going to be a mom. The betrayal of the girl she thought was her friend, felt like a slap in the face, as a weight settled in her chest. She whirled on Trina and shot her an icy stare.

"Last summer, when we talked on the phone, and I told you I couldn't go with you to Florida, you knew why. You knew I was pregnant, and I told you Brady was the father and that I had feelings for him. You even encouraged me to contact him. That I had to let him know." She walked toward Trina. Her steps were sharp and intentional. "Why would you invite him down to be with you if you knew I was going to talk with him? If you knew there was a chance he and I might end up together?"

Trina turned her head toward the ceiling. Her face was emotionless. "Look, it's not a big deal. Like Brady said, you two weren't a thing. You hadn't talked to him, yet. How was I supposed to know that when you did talk to him, all of this would come about?" She motioned between Elizabeth and Brady and Grant.

Trina sauntered to Brady's side and rubbed his arm. "Don't get mad at him. He wasn't thinking about you at all during that time. I was the only person on his mind, and in his bed that weekend and the rest of the summer. Wasn't I Brady?"

Brady's eyes shot toward Trina's like a torpedo. Elizabeth gasped at the emotional slap she experienced.

She shot over to Trina, whose hand was still on Brady's arm. "Take your hand off him, and you better leave. I don't think we need to spend any more time together. Get the hell out of my house, Trina!" Elizabeth spat these words from behind closed teeth. Her eyes threw daggers, and her heart felt like it was beating out of her chest. Trina did not move her body or her hand, so Elizabeth grabbed her hand and yanked it from Brady. "Take. Your hand. Off him. And leave my house!"

Trina threw her hands up in mock defeat. "Fine. I'm leaving. Even though I don't know why you're getting so worked up about this." Trina winked at Brady and let herself out the front door.

Elizabeth stared at the front door. Her heart was still pounding like it needed to be set free. She grasped her hands behind her head, intertwining her fingers. Taking some deep breaths to calm her heart and pulse, she closed her eyes.

Did Trina just seem proud of the fact that she slept with Brady after I told her about the baby? Did Brady really try to shove it under the rug? Her blood grew hot as the reality of what had transpired rushed through her. She concentrated on her breathing. *In through the nose.* She took a deep breath in. *Out through the mouth.* She slowly pushed it out.

She turned toward Brady and watched him watch her. The silence was as thick as some of the crap in Grant's diapers.

"Well? What the hell was that all about?" She grabbed her son out of his arms. "You never thought it was important enough to tell me about your and Trina's 'thing' last summer?"

"Elizabeth, I—"

Her pulse raced. She held up her hand, closing her eyes to help block out the excuse getting ready to pour from his mouth. Her eyes got wide as she flashed back to last fall when she met Brady to tell him about the pregnancy. He mentioned going to Florida. But nothing significant.

"Wait a minute. Why did this not come up when we talked about our summer last year? You just told me you went with Trent to Florida. Wouldn't that have been a perfect time to tell me about you and Trina? Why did you hide it from me?"

Brady's gaze flitted quickly toward the door, then slowly back on Elizabeth. Her insides churned again, this time worse than before. She really did think she might be sick. Part of her wanted to stop the questioning and just ignore it, but the rational side of her heart, the side which at times like this she really hated, wouldn't let it go. She laid the sleeping baby gently in his playpen to free up her arms, making it easier to talk.

"Was there more between you two than just a one-night stand? Now would be a perfect time to tell all. Trina made it seem like there was." She willed her eyes to stay on him so he would have to talk.

Brady's eyes filled with tears, guilty tears. His face drooped under the pressure and finally, so did his gaze. "Elizabeth, I love you. I've always loved you, but I was stupid. Last summer, my goal was to forget about you. I could have called you, but I don't know." He fell onto the sofa with his hands covering his face, his fingers gripping in his hair.

"I went to Florida and was excited about seeing her again, and yes, a part of me was hoping that you'd be there. But Trina told me you were busy with a new life and a new guy and decided to stay at home. I wondered then why was I waiting for you? If I wanted you so bad, I would have just called." Elizabeth gasped as hurt sliced through her heart. "So yes, I was with Trina, and we had a relationship going all summer. I went down and saw her a couple of times. She came to see me. Until you called, and we started talking." He looked up at Elizabeth.

He knelt in front of her and took her hands in his. He brushed her knuckles softly with his lips. His voice became soft and filled with emotion. "I know I should have mentioned her before this, and I'm so sorry you found out this way, but you need to know I love you. You and Grant have my heart. I need you both in my life." Her hazel eyes were shining with unshed tears.

"Elizabeth, there's nothing between Trina and me now. It's just you. I swear." He stretched himself up and pulled her to his mouth. He kissed her, and when she started to respond, he slowly rose to his feet, pulling her up with him.

Brady broke their kiss and held her tight against him. "I'm so sorry, Elizabeth. I hurt you. I never want to see that look in your eyes again. I'll be honest with you from now on. I promise. Are we okay?"

Elizabeth searched his face. He looked sincere. She couldn't really blame him for being with Trina. When they left college, she told him they were over. A small smile grew on her lips. She nodded and leaned in softly, pressing her mouth to his. Something within her wasn't sure if she should let him off so easily, but again, the irrational part of her heart spoke for her. She gave in to him, body and soul. She melted against him, wanting to show him he didn't need anyone but her.

She led him to the couch, lowering him onto it with her kisses. She straddled his lap, unbuttoned her blouse, and slipped it from her arms. She let her bra fall to the floor and placed his hands over her breasts.

He kneaded and kissed her where she wanted him to—needed him to. His kisses left her breast and trailed up her neck. He held her head in his hands and forced her eyes to look at him.

"I promise you, Elizabeth, I love you. There is only you. Like I said before, you and Grant have my heart. Please say you believe me."

She searched his eyes, and her heart skipped a beat. "I do. I believe you. I love you so much."

Elizabeth closed her eyes and tilted her head back in ecstasy as his mouth closed once again over her breast. Somehow, he freed his hardness from its captivity and lifted her skirt just enough. She lowered her body onto him until he filled her. She leaned in to kiss him and felt his tension release.

Chapter 18

The crash of pins and cheers of celebration greeted them when Jessica and Elizabeth entered the bowling alley after work. They found Brady and Chad easily. Kristen and Jacob were there with Stacey. Elizabeth stopped. She wasn't in the mood to deal with Kristen's attitude tonight. She blew out a breath.

Jessica glanced at her and pulled her along. "I thought you two were good."

Elizabeth kept her gaze straight ahead. "Yeah, well, we're better. But you know she's Kristen."

"Come on. She'll be fine. Jacob keeps her toned down a notch."

Elizabeth pushed her eyebrows up, doubting Jessica's words. "Yeah, we'll see. I promise I'll be nice—or as nice as humanly possible." She forced a smile on her face as they approached the lane.

Brady met her and wrapped her in his tight, protective hug that she loved. Their lips met each other before he pulled away. "How was work?" He pushed a stray piece of hair from her face.

"Good. Busy. The online store went live today, and it really made it easy for customers to purchase items. Mrs. Stanzel seems pleased." Elizabeth was proud. She set out to do something and it was a success—more so than she anticipated. Her heart was full. She ran her hands through his thick wavy hair. "So, how was your day? Is that project almost done?"

"Well, it's almost finished, but it seems like we may have to work all next weekend." Elizabeth's good mood fell. She was hoping for a weekend with Brady and Grant. There was a festival on Main Street, and she wanted them to go. To have some family time.

He continued. "I've already cleared it with Chad, not that he has any say over what Jessica does, and I talked to your mom. I thought that if you and Jessica wanted to, you could both spend the weekend in Nashville or the mountains. I know you've been talking about going on a girls' weekend. If you want, I can book you a room. I'm sure you two would have fun wherever you go. Maybe you could even invite Stacey and Kristen. You know, make it a real girls' weekend."

Elizabeth grabbed his arm and studied his face. She hadn't had a chance to get away in a while and could use some girl time but including Kristen? Really? "That sounds amazing. But with Kristen? I know we're doing better, but I'm not sure about spending a weekend with her."

He smiled a wide toothy grin. "Yes, include Kristen. It would be good for her. And you."

As quickly as a smile was on her face, it fell. "I don't know about leaving Grant for the weekend. You'd be working. Are my parents good with watching him?"

Brady slowly nodded. "Yes, I told you I already talked to them. I'll have him on Friday. They'll get him at night. I promise I will check in regularly." He pulled her closer, wrapping his arms around her. "It's not fair for you to always be at home watching Grant. You go have fun with the girls."

A thoughtful look passed over Elizabeth's face, which made him throw his head back in laughter. "I'm serious. Go and have fun." He gestured to the group they were bowling with.

They walked toward the crowd. "It does sound like it would be a good time, except for Kristen coming along." Brady raised his eyebrow. "Look, I'm trying to work things out between us. She just makes things difficult."

She walked up to Stacey, and gave her a hug, got a high-five from Chad, and a nod and a smile from Jacob. Kristen just shot her a look. Typical.

The girls sat out the next game, deciding instead to relax at a table, drink, and heckle the guys as they played for pride and money—the loser having to foot the bar tab for the night. Last month it was Chad who lost, mainly because he drank too much to begin with, but this time he came prepared and stayed mostly sober.

Filling her cup with beer, yet again, the alcohol giving her the courage she needed to deal with Kristen, Elizabeth turned and looked directly at her. The other two girls gave their full attention to the conversation at the table instead of the game in front of them.

"Okay, Kristen. I thought we'd already cleared things up. Why do we still have to do this? It's getting really old, and I'm tired of fighting with you. You know how Jacob feels about you. I'd love for us to all just be friends."

Kristen narrowed her steel-blue eyes into slits and brushed her hair back. "What? Why would I do that? Every chance you get, you flirt with my boyfriend. You use that son of yours to get him to spend time with you. It's sad. I feel sorry for you."

Stacey gasped and draped her arm over Kristen's shoulder, hugging her close. "Come on already. My brother helped out with Grant once when Elizabeth was in the hospital. We had fun. You might've enjoyed it. He is such a cute little boy."

Kristen scrunched her mouth. "Babies are gross. They're all slobber and shit." She shuddered, making laughter ring around the table.

"Oh, come on, Kristen. You don't think his little smile and laugh are adorable?" asked Jessica, trying to calm her laughter.

Kristen rolled her eyes as the guys finally joined them. Jacob and Chad had smiles plastered on their faces while they surrounded Brady, whose head was down, grimacing.

"You girls missed an epic ending." Chad pulled a chair up between Jessica and Elizabeth and placed a big, loud kiss on Jessica's lips. She batted him away with a smile. "Elizabeth, I'm sorry to say, but your man's bank account will be getting quite a bit smaller. He lost by five pins."

Jacob sat by Kristen, placing his arm over her shoulder. "Yeah, he did. So close, yet nothing. I, on the other hand..." He stopped and looked at Kristen. "Still undefeated." He winked at her at gave her an enormous smile.

"And the hottest bowler here." Kristen finished and leaned

toward him to claim him with a kiss.

"Okay, enough of this mushy stuff." Brady gestured toward the empty pitcher. "I'll go get another pitcher or two for the table and drop off my card." He puffed out his chest. "At least my bank account is good for it." He squeezed Elizabeth's shoulder as he walked away.

Elizabeth brought up the idea of a girls' weekend. She told them about the room Brady would get them. All they had to do was decide where they wanted to go. She pushed for the mountains. Shopping and hiking seemed like a perfect getaway.

"What do y'all think? Jessica, Chad already okayed for you to go."

Jessica glared at her boyfriend. "Really, you gave the okay for me. Like you own me, huh?" She laughed but was interrupted as Brady passed out shots to everyone and placed the beer on the table.

Chad ran his fingers through a lock of Jessica's hair. "Well, I'm hoping I will—sort of, anyway." Chad got out of his chair, flattened out his shirt with his hands, and looked around. He picked up his beer and took a swig, then breathed in a big breath, blowing it out slowly.

"Jessica..." He pulled her to her feet.

Confusion and shock became plastered on her face. Jessica looked up into the eyes of the handsome six-foot-five man in front of her. His dirty-blond hair was slightly messed up, and his gray eyes shined with nervousness—A look no one was used to seeing on him.

She bit her lip. "Chad, what..."

He placed his hand over her mouth and shook his head to quiet her. "This isn't the romantic proposal you want or deserve, but our friends are here."

Chad dropped to his knee, and Jessica's eyes grew as wide as dinner plates.

Reaching into his pocket, he pulled out a ring, and made eye contact with this girl he loved. "Jess, I love you. I love who I am when I'm with you, and nothing would make me happier than if you would say yes and marry me."

Jessica brought both her hands to her mouth as she started shaking, and tears streamed down her face. She nodded and started to bounce up and down.

"Thank God." Chad bowed his head for a second before he stood up and put his arms around Jessica. "You were taking so long; I was scared you were going to say no."

Jessica laughed at him. "Of course not. I would never say no to you." She held her left hand toward him, and Chad placed the ring on her finger.

"I love you, Jess." Chad's smile filled his face.

"I love you too, Chad." Jessica jumped into his arms and placed a kiss on his lips. Everyone around the table, and others in the bowling alley, cheered.

Elizabeth's heart swelled. She wrapped Jessica in a huge congratulatory hug, squeezing her hard.

"This calls for a toast." Brady started handing out shots. "To the happy couple, Jessica and Chad."

"To Jessica and Chad." Echoed around as everyone turned

back their shot glasses, Jessica and Elizabeth grimaced at the taste of tequila as it slid down their throats and quickly chased it with a mouth full of beer.

Chapter 19

Elizabeth was enjoying her morning coffee on the back patio, watching Grant play in his exersaucer, when her phone rang, cutting through the peaceful atmosphere like a knife slicing through a cake. She didn't recognize the number and considered ignoring it but picked it up anyway.

She should have ignored it. It was Trina.

"I know you don't want to talk to me but hear me out. Please?"

Elizabeth cleared her throat, pulled the phone away from her ear, and hit speaker. If she was going to talk to Trina, she wouldn't give her the courtesy of holding the phone to her ear.

"What do you want Trina? I'm busy." Elizabeth rose from her chair and picked up Grant. It was too nice a day to sit here watching the sun wake up. She wanted to take a walk and needed to stop in the boutique. Walking to the store would help her get exercise and walk off the stress of dealing with this phone call.

"I'm sure you are, but I'd love to meet you for lunch today in town. I'm going back and don't want to leave things how they are between us."

"How are things between us?" Elizabeth felt her blood pressure rising. What more did she have to say to her? Did she not get the message when she kicked her out of her house? Elizabeth snapped Grant in the stroller, handed him his favorite stuffed animal to gnaw on, and set out through the gate, the phone still on speaker.

Trina sighed into the phone. "Please, just meet me, and let's talk. Can you meet me for pizza at noon?"

She knew she should tell Trina to screw off and leave her and her family alone. Sometimes she was just too nice. "Fine, but I'll have Grant with me, so I won't be able to stay long. I can eat and leave."

"Great! See you then." Trina hung up.

"Wow, Grant. I guess we have a lunch date with Trina. Can't wait."

Elizabeth entered the door of the boutique with Grant in her arms and walked through the store. She found her boss stocking shelves in the back corner. "Hi, Mrs. Stanzel."

Barbara, surprised, looked up and smiled. "Hi! What brings you by?"

Elizabeth held up a finger. "I'll be right back." She placed a sleeping Grant in his playpen in the back office and turned on the baby monitor she had sitting on her desk, clipping the portable half to her pants, and returned to her boss.

"Why are you doing this? What happened to the girl you just hired?" She asked.

"Well, she didn't show up yesterday, and when she was late today, I called her. She said she couldn't come to work anymore. She found a better-paying job. Just decided to not show up."

Elizabeth's mouth dropped open. "Oh, my gosh. That's the second one in just as many months. What's going on with people?"

Mrs. Stanzel waved her hand to brush off the remark. "It doesn't matter. I told her that I'd have her last paycheck here for her whenever she wanted to pick it up. I put it in the drawer. I'm interested in seeing how long it will be until she comes and gets it."

Excitement flooded Elizabeth. "Mrs. Stanzel. I know just the person!" She turned quickly, knocking over open boxes, their contents pouring out onto the floor.

Mrs. Stanzel jumped. "Goodness!" Her hand flew to her heart.

"Sorry." Elizabeth bit her bottom lip, trying to restrain the smile that threatened to appear as she picked up the items that spilled onto the floor. She was glad nothing was breakable. "Would you be interested in hiring someone else? I know someone looking for a job."

"Well, I did want to talk to you and get your thoughts about someone. I have a friend's daughter who I'd like to start working a couple hours Tuesday through Thursday and Fridays and Saturdays all day. She's pregnant, so there will be times when she needs time off. If you'd be available those days to fill in, that would be great. She's a wonderful girl and excited about getting started. I know you don't want to work a lot, but it's just to fill in for her occasionally. What do you think?"

"Wow, that's weird. The person I was going to ask you to hire is pregnant. Her name's Leila Jones."

Mrs. Stanzel laughed. "Well, seems as if great minds think alike. That's who I'm hiring."

Elizabeth felt a wave of relief wash over her. "I'm so glad she has a job. She's such a sweet girl, but I'm not sure I'll be able to work more. I won't have my mom or Joanna to babysit on other days."

"Grant's always welcome here. You know that."

"I know, but I can focus so much better if he's not here, but if I can't find someone, he'll just have to come with me."

Working together, they finished replenishing the stock. "Well, I'm gonna go work on the website. I have some updates to make." Elizabeth excused herself and went to the office.

Elizabeth worked quietly while Grant napped. The changes she made to the website looked good. She sat up taller and stretched as she clicked through the pages. Her eyes flicked to the clock at the bottom of the computer screen. Whoa! A jolt shot through her. She had been working longer than she thought. Only twenty minutes until she had to meet Trina.

Elizabeth was logging off the computer, and cleaning up her desk when Barbara came in.

"I'm glad I stopped in today, but I need to get going. I'm seeing a friend for lunch."

Barbara leaned over the playpen. "He is such a handsome little thing. I'm serious, Elizabeth. If you can't find someone to watch him, please bring him with you. We'll set up an area for him to play."

Picking up her son, Elizabeth raised an eyebrow. "If You're serious." She bounced him gently as he started to wake up and suck on his fingers.

Mrs. Stanzel rubbed his head and cheek. "I would love nothing more than to have this handsome guy in my store. He's such an angel."

Elizabeth laughed. "Yeah, well, he does have his moments. I promise." Elizabeth placed him in his stroller and toward the pizza place. Dread crept throughout her body the closer she got to the restaurant. Now would be a great time for Grant to get grumpy. It would give her a reason to bail. *Stop thinking that way, Elizabeth. You got this. Don't let her get to you. She's not worth it.*

Chapter 20

"I'll have a pepperoni pizza, some garlic knots, a side salad and some water, please." Elizabeth gave her order to the server and played with Grant as she waited for Trina.

"Grant, maybe she changed her mind and decided to bail because she can't face me." Grant smiled and gave his mom a little laugh as he banged his plastic spoon on the table, then put it in his mouth.

"Hi there, little man."

Trina arrived. Damn. She didn't bail. Elizabeth shot her a fake smile.

Trina was dressed casually in a crop top and light sweater, with a short skirt. The most conservative Elizabeth remembers ever seeing her. She brushed her hand over Grant's dark little curls as she sat at the table. "What a cutie. You look so much like your daddy."

Grant giggled at Trina and blew his standard raspberry. Elizabeth's stomach curdled.

Trina laughed. "Elizabeth, he is just adorable."

"Thanks." *Why did I agree to this lunch?* She picked up her water and took a drink. "Trina, what's up with *you*? I don't think you asked me here for lunch just to hang out. Since you showed up, it seems like you've been trying to start problems between me and Brady. I'm sure you'll be glad to finally get back to Florida. Why do you keep stalling?"

Trina placed her well-manicured hands on the table and interlaced her fingers. "Well, I won't be going back as soon as I hoped, and I just felt bad with how things ended at your place."

The knot in Elizabeth's stomach morphed into a stone. What now? What could she possibly be up to? She chose her words carefully for fear she might jump across the table and tear Trina limb from limb. "What do you mean you won't be going back? That's always been your goal. Living in Florida, sun, parties..." She had to swallow...hard.

"My dad isn't doing well, so my mom asked me to come home for a bit. Since I'll be around for a while, I thought maybe we could fix things between us. You and Brady are the only friends I have here. All my old friends have moved away, or we just lost touch."

Did her friends really lose touch, or did she treat them as bitchy as she treated Elizabeth? Lies. Betrayal. All great ingredients to being a loyal friend. "Okay, well, Trina, I find it hard to think you wanted me to have lunch with you so you could tell me this. What else do you need to talk about?"

Trina sat up tall and rigid, giving Elizabeth a smirk. "You know, I felt bad for how I left your house the other day. I'm so sorry that Brady wasn't honest with you. It put our friendship in a stressful situation. I've never hidden anything from you in the past, and I have the feeling that you think I am now. Look, I'm glad you and Brady have worked things out, and I sure don't want to get in the way if you have a healthy relationship."

A healthy relationship! Is she serious? Elizabeth took a deep breath and counted to ten. "We do have a healthy relationship."

"Yeah..." Trina glanced at Elizabeth over her glass of sweet tea. "Everyone can see how crazy you are for him, and he seems that way about you, too. And this little boy here, wow! So cute!"

The food Elizabeth ordered arrived. She tore the doughy inside of a garlic knot into pieces for Grant to eat. "Trina, can I ask you a question?"

"Of course."

"Why'd you invite Brady down to Florida and start something while you were encouraging me to talk with him? That's really disingenuous."

Trina's eyes became innocent as she snagged a slice of pizza. "Look, Elizabeth, I didn't really think you were going to contact him."

Elizabeth cocked her head.

"Really. It's true. As soon as I found out, I stepped aside and let him make the first move."

"What does that mean?" Elizabeth's mouth fell open and the stone in her stomach multiplied. "You weren't together after he was in the hospital last summer, were you?"

"Together, then? No. He did have to come to Florida one last time. He had some of my stuff, and I had some of his. That's how he found out what size ring you wore. He came down, and we went out shopping just to pass some time. I found a ring I liked and just happened to tell him that you and I wear the same size." Trina took a big bite of pizza and chased it with sweet tea, taking her time before speaking again. "The next time I talked to him was when he called me to ask about my size. He told me he was going to propose. We talked for a while. He asked me to stop in for a visit whenever I went home. I came home to visit and had an invite from both of you."

Elizabeth froze. "Brady talked to you and invited you over? Why would he not have told me? He sounded surprised when I said something to him about it." *What else is going on?* She placed her hands over her stomach as the pizza threatened to show itself again. "Trina..."

Trina lifted an eyebrow and held Elizabeth's gaze as a smile crept slowly across her lips.

This isn't the whole story. Brady needs to do some explaining. Elizabeth just shook her head. "Nothing. Forget about it."

"Well," Trina stood up." "This has been fun, but I've gotta run." She went to Elizabeth and gave her a hug. She brushed down Grant's hair. "Bye, little one. I'm sure I'll see you again soon. Later. Liz." She waved and left.

Elizabeth followed the witch with her eyes. *Why is she really here? What is going on with her and Brady, and why did she say* if *we had a healthy relationship?*

Grant squealed. She brushed her hands along her son's curls. "Everything's good with me and your daddy, Grant." Staring at her son, she willed the rock in her stomach to go away. She leaned gently against his head, breathing in his scent to calm her frayed nerves.

"Do you mind if I take a seat?" Kristen motioned to the empty chair just vacated by Trina. The irony of one friend turning enemy leaving, and one enemy trying to become a friend staying, was not lost on Elizabeth. Elizabeth kissed Grant and motioned to the chair.

Kristen sat and fidgeted with the fork that was lying on the table.

"What brings you by?" Elizabeth picked up another piece of pizza, giving her crust to Grant and laughed softly as he used it as a hammer.

Kristen looked around uneasily. "Well, I'm meeting Jacob here for lunch. I saw you here and thought, why not? We are trying to get along, and it would make him happy if he saw me sitting with you."

Elizabeth laughed. Only Kristen would think that was a good-hearted reason to do something, but at the same time, it probably seemed like a way for her to stay in the good graces of her boyfriend. "Okay, well, we will see what he thinks." She waved across the restaurant. "Here he is now."

Jacob walked over to the table and went to Grant first. Giving him a little pat of acknowledgment. Grant blew raspberries mixed with pizza crust crumbs in reply. He then greeted Elizabeth with a hug before he sat next to Kristen and placed a soft kiss on her lips.

They really did seem happy. She was glad. She also noticed she had no pangs of jealousy or longing inside her, either. She smiled. Her feelings had moved on from Jacob.

Jacob looked between the two girls and back at Kristen,

grabbing a bite of her pizza. Elizabeth offered up what was left of her and Trina's, so he helped himself.

"Okay, not gonna lie, but I am very shocked to see you two sitting here together. I know you've been working on this friend thing but it hasn't really been going great." Jacob spoke between bites of pizza.

Elizabeth lifted her eyes.

"Alright, Elizabeth, not you as much as Kristen."

Kristen rolled her eyes and looked at the ceiling. "Look, you asked me to try to get a long and give her a break. So here I am." She glanced at Jacob. "Anyway, when I got here, she was in an intense conversation with that friend of hers from college. What's her name? Terry... Traci...."

Why did she have to see that? Elizabeth uttered between clenched teeth. "Trina."

"Yeah, that's it. Trina. So, I wanted to come and see if everything was good."

"Thanks, Kristen." Elizabeth sighed and slouched in her seat, resting her head in her hand. "It was nice of you to stop over and check on me. That wasn't the best lunch meeting I ever had."

"Yeah, it didn't seem like it was going well. You looked irritated and a little upset." Kristen continued eating.

"Is everything okay?" Jacob asked.

Elizabeth nodded. "Yeah, I guess sometimes it's hard realizing you've moved on from some friendships." She wiped away the thought, and they ate in silence.

"Hey, Kristen, I don't know if you remember our talk of a

girls' weekend when we were bowling, but Jessica, Stacey, and I decided on this weekend. We're leaving Friday for Gatlinburg and getting back Sunday. Shopping, dancing, drinking, guys."

Jacob froze with his pizza on the way to his mouth and popped an eyebrow.

Elizabeth laughed. "Just kidding, Jacob. Absolutely no guys. Would you like to join us, Kristen? It'll be fun. All girl time without guys in the way. Brady's already paid for the hotel."

Shock was evident on Jacob's face when he turned to Kristen. "You know, Kris, I think that would be good for you. Go ahead. Get away with the girls."

Kristen looked at him wide-eyed. "You want me to go? Are you sure?"

Jacob laughed and placed his arm around her shoulder, pulling her toward him. "Of course, I'm sure. It'll give me and Chad a chance to hang with Brady more. We can have a guy's weekend of sorts. Party, strippers. You know, guy stuff."

Kristen's eyes went wide. Jacob gave her chin a nudge. "Just kidding, Kris. You're cute when you're jealous!" He gave her a peck on the nose.

Chapter 21

As Elizabeth got closer to home, her uneasiness crept back in, and she felt sick to her stomach. Brady's constant dishonesty gnawed at her. Why didn't he just come clean with everything that happened between him and Trina?

"Grant, what are we going to do? Am I overreacting?" Suddenly a car horn honked as she was crossing the road to their townhouse. Her face filled with surprise when she saw that it was Brady. He pulled the car into the garage. Elizabeth and Grant joined him.

He quickly wrapped her in an enormous hug, smiling from ear to ear. "Got off early and wanted to get home to surprise my favorite people."

"What happened to working late?"

He leaned down to give her a kiss, and she turned her cheek toward his lips, her mind still on her discussion with Trina.

Brady looked down at her. "It was postponed. Hey, beautiful. Is something wrong?"

Elizabeth turned away and shook her head. She picked Grant up from his stroller, carried him into the house, and sat him in his play pen.

He followed and tugged her around to face him enveloping

her in his arms. "Not so fast. I need to know what's wrong. You usually give me a kiss."

She peered at him and felt anger rising in her chest. "You do realize, that not telling me something is just as bad as lying about it, right?"

Brady tilted his head and shook it in confusion. "I don't know what you're talking about."

Her blood started to pound in her head. She pulled away from his embrace, and leaned on the kitchen counter, looking blindly at the floor, not wanting to meet his eyes. "What else is there between you and Trina that I don't know about?"

Brady chewed on his bottom lip and averted his eyes away from Elizabeth. She sighed deeply and rubbed her face in her hands. "I had lunch with her today, and she was filled with all kinds of interesting information." Elizabeth's neck started getting hot. She gave it a massage.

"You told me you ended things with her once we started talking. But according to Trina, you did see her again. And you talked to her since then. You called her to ask about my ring size. You invited her to visit if she went to see her parents. Why didn't you tell me that?"

Realization washed over Brady. "Liz, I'm sorry. I didn't think it was a big deal. Really, I didn't. I went back down to Florida to pick up some of my things. That's it."

"She liked you in college. She was always jealous of us. I think she still has those feelings, and since you were together last summer, it just makes them more intense." She finally met his gaze, hers filled with unshed tears. "You've got to understand, you can't be just friends with her. That's not what she wants. It won't work between us if you're friends with her." Her heart was beating so fast, she thought it might explode. She tried to take deep breaths to calm her nerves, but it didn't seem to work.

Brady rolled his eyes toward the ceiling. "Elizabeth, now you're being ridiculous and jealous. You and Jacob are still friends. I'm okay with it."

"It's not the same. Jacob and I were a quick fling. You and Trina were together a lot over a long period." She turned her back on Brady and stared out the window. Why can't he see the difference? Trina's out for Trina. Jacob has moved on. He's not trying to get back with me.

His voice rose in tone and got louder. "A quick fling? Really?" He raked his fingers through his hair and held on to his hair in fistfuls. Taking a deep breath, he let it all go, bringing his hands to his chest. "I don't recall that I ever left you at dinner to make out with Trina. I seem to remember catching you lip locked in the parking lot with Jacob and upset that he walked away choosing to stay with Kristen." Brady grabbed her and flung her around to face him again. Hurt and fury filled his eyes.

Elizabeth fell over her words. "Okay, yeah, I screwed up that one time. But you and Trina were...," she waved her hand in the air. "Whatever you were."

"You're still being ridiculous." Brady turned his back to her, putting some space between them and clasped his hands behind his neck.

Elizabeth's pulse rose as she walked around in front of him, needing to see his face. She took a deep breath and forced her voice to remain calm. "How would you feel if I was 'hanging out,' and 'just friends' with Trent? Would that make you feel good seeing me with someone I slept with a lot during college?"

Brady's eyes narrowed. She could see the rise and fall of his chest speed up. "See, it would bother you. That's how I feel about you and Trina, except you couldn't leave Trina alone. You were so interested in her, that you went back to her all summer long, even after we started talking."

Her calm demeanor started cracking, and her voice became harsh. "And you kept it from me." She pushed his chest. "You lied about things, and now I find out she told you about my ring size, and all you said was you can't 'reveal all your secrets.' Really. What other secrets do you have, Brady? She wouldn't still be here if she felt you were one hundred percent invested in us." Elizabeth pushed on his chest harder.

He stumbled back slightly. He held her stare, his breath coming fast before he finally looked away and pushed out a big breath.

Elizabeth's stomach flopped and raging butterflies invaded it. He's always breathed hard when there is something he needed to say. What more could it be? She took a deep, shaky breath and swallowed down the lump in her throat. Her voice became calmer, softer. She placed her hand on his cheek and guided his face toward hers again. "I feel like there is still something you're not telling me. What is it, Brady?"

She searched his eyes, trying to dig out what she wasn't sure she wanted to find, but what she knew he was hiding deep in his soul. She cupped his face and leaned in, brushing her lips against his. When she pulled away, she waited until his eyes fluttered open. "Brady, you're scaring me. Please talk to me."

He placed his hands on her arms and rubbed gently up and down. His face pleaded with her. But why?

"I love you so much, Elizabeth." He took another big breath, trying to hold back the tears which threatened to fall.

Elizabeth was frozen in place. His tears filled her heart with dread. *What have you done, Brady? Don't say it.* She covered her face with her hands, willing her pulse to slow and her breathing to calm.

Fear greeted her. She backed away from him and lowered herself onto a chair at the table.

Brady's gaze found hers and pleaded for forgiveness before the words were formed. "Elizabeth, I'm so sorry."

His face fell apart like a tree losing its leaves in the fall. One hand covered his mouth as the other reached toward her. He kneeled on the floor, his head falling in Elizabeth's lap. He wrapped his free arm around his son and Elizabeth. Elizabeth felt his embrace become tighter. Her breathing halted, and her hand went to his shoulder, giving him a small shove so she could see his face. Her eyes were like two stones, cold and hard, and they forced him to continue.

"The night… you were in your accident…"

Elizabeth pushed him off her, and she jumped up. Her head tilted to the side, her eyes still wide as she clasped desperately onto her son, who squirmed in her arms. The look she saw on Brady's face scarred her soul. Her worst fear became a reality.

Brady stayed where he was, leaning against the chair she had just vacated. He focused on the seat in front of him. "I was with Trina... she came by the office." He slowly lifted his face. Elizabeth shot angry straight into his soul. He slumped in defeat.

Elizabeth opened her mouth to speak, but nothing came out. She couldn't make sense of the feelings churning inside of her. Hurt. Sadness. Anger. She turned and walked out of the kitchen to the couch. Her legs finally gave out, and she fell onto the cushions. Brady sat down cautiously next to her. When he opened his mouth to talk, Elizabeth held her hand in the air, stopping his words.

She stood up and gently laid Grant in his playpen, covering him with his blanket. Her hand hesitated for a moment on Grant's back. Watching him fall asleep helped to focus her and calmed her.

Slowly, she turned to face Brady. "What do you mean you were"—she curled her fingers in the air—'with' Trina?" She tried to stay calm.

His inability to keep his face on hers answered for him.

"Did you fuck her? Is that what you meant?" She spit out the words in a harsh whisper. She tried to stay calm but failed miserably. Her pulse raced like a horse on the track.

He gazed blindly across the room and slumped against the back of the couch and stayed quiet.

She saw red,

"How could you?" Her voice became louder, harsher.

His voice was small but desperate. "Elizabeth, I'm so sorry! It was a huge mistake. I know that and I wish I could take it back. I've talked with her since then and told her it won't happen again. Ever." He closed the space between them and clasped her hands in his. "Please believe me. I love you so much."

She felt numb as her eyes got as wide as saucers. "Don't. Use. Those. Words!" Elizabeth jerked her hands from his, trying hard to keep her voice calm, not wanting to scare Grant. "If you really loved me, you wouldn't have sex with another woman." She walked away from him to the desk in the corner. "I can't believe this. I ..." She braced her hands on the surface and took deep breaths, trying to control her urge to break something and to scream. She took a deep cleansing breath in through her nostrils and blew it out slowly, hanging her head low. "Since she's been here, how many times have you fucked her?"

Silence.

Her pulse quickened. Her voice got louder, and she enunciated each word. "Brady. How. Many. Times?"

She felt a light touch on her arm. His touch sent a shock through her, but she resisted the desire to flinch away.

"Only that once. I promise." His voice was quiet and beat down.

Now she flinched. Just enough, so his touch no longer singed her insides. A knot of disappointment lodged itself inside her. She felt sick and swallowed down that knot rising in her chest.

Memories of late work nights came flooding back to her. Her eyes flew open, and she turned on him, knocking him backward. "Why should I believe you?" She yelled.

He stumbled back. His hands held up to ward off her wrath as she confronted him face-to-face.

"Those late nights you had, you weren't working, were you?" She screamed as her heart thumped desperately in her chest.

His hands fell to his side. "Liz, yes. I was working. I only had sex with her once since last summer. You've got to believe me."

Elizabeth stopped as she felt her heart break. Her insides were a mess of emotions that, when thrown together, were almost unbearable. She shook her head as disappointment and disbelief engulfed her. She covered her face with her hands. Why? Why did her past have to keep messing up the present? Why didn't she believe him? Why couldn't he be faithful?

She talked through her hands. "Only once? You say that like it's okay. Only once. And then, to top it off, it was the night I could have died, and you weren't there. You were with her!" She took a deep breath, forced her breathing to calm, and stretched her neck. She looked at him and pushed her shoulders back. "Why couldn't you be happy with me and Grant?" She uncovered her face, meeting his eyes. "You wanted this." She waved her hands between them. "You said you loved me. Please, what else do you need to tell me? I know there's more. Come clean now."

Elizabeth stared hot coals at him. She refused to back down.

The feeling that there was more was so strong she could touch it.

Brady shook his head. "I promise. It didn't happen again, even though she tried."

Elizabeth's body folded. She was exhausted. Her voice was almost a whisper. "What do you mean she tried?"

"God, Liz." Brady stopped and took a deep breath. "There were a lot of texts. She tried to get me to see her, and when I wouldn't, it's what I already told you. She came to the house. She tried to kiss me the first night she was here in our garage and again in the kitchen the day you came home. I told her I love you, and she needed to stop."

Elizabeth's face fell and she looked anywhere but at the man in front of her. She didn't think she could feel anything worse than what she felt earlier, but she was wrong. Finally, she turned toward him. Even though it was difficult, she forced herself to keep her eyes on his. "Do you even know how to love someone, or can you only be selfish and think of yourself?" She paused waiting for a response, but was met with a blank, tear-filled stare.

"Just so you know, messing around on the person you say you love, isn't how you love someone." She stopped and breathed. "You want her? Guess what? You can have her. Get away from me."

Brady's look became desperate. "Elizabeth, please. I told you—"

"I don't care what you told me." She was losing control, and anger took over her body. "I can't trust anything you say.

You said you love me. You said you want to be with me." She calmed down.

She slowly walked toward him and touched his face again and let out a long sigh. She could feel her anger causing the well inside her to fill up, but she didn't want to cry in front of him. Not again.

Holding his gaze, she talked in a much more confident voice than she felt. "I need to go. You need to figure out who you want. I need to figure out if I still want you. I'm gonna take Grant and go to my parents'."

Without looking back, Elizabeth rushed up the steps, grabbed Grant's diaper bag, his favorite stuffed animal and blanket and shoved in some clothes. Then she went to her room and stuffed clothes and shoes with her makeup in a duffle bag. For now, this would be enough.

With the bags slung over her shoulder, she walked into the living room where Brady stood over Grant's playpen. He turned toward her, his eyes swimming with tears. She drank in his profile and got lost in his brown eyes once more. When he started becoming blurry, she picked up Grant and his diaper bag, grabbed her purse, and slammed the door behind her.

Chapter 22

Brady stood in silence, frozen. The tears which fell down his face, cut into his soul like a knife. He shook his head as he slowly walked through the empty house. Stupid. God, you're stupid.

He stopped at Grant's bedroom door and leaned on the door frame. He took in the room, filled with trucks, blocks, and stuffed animals. "God, Brady, you were happy. Why did you have to screw it up?" He put his hands behind his head and squeezed his fingers into his hair. The tears finally stopped, and he felt numb. He walked down the hall to his and Elizabeth's bedroom, trying not to look around too much. He would see her everywhere.

He grabbed his duffle bag and quickly threw a few pieces of clothing inside, picked up his phone and stared at the screen at a text that must have come in when he was talking with Elizabeth.

What the hell? Why won't she get the message? "Don't make another dumb decision. You'll never be able to get her back."

Sighing deeply, he shook his head and dialed. "I need you to come get me. I don't think it's safe for me to drive, and I can't stay in this house tonight." He nodded to the phone as if the person on the other side could see him and hung up.

It was a long twenty minutes as Brady sat on the front porch steps waiting for the car to pull up and take him away from his house, from his screw up. He sat with his head in his hands, slumped forward. "Brady, you're such an idiot!"

Finally, headlights turned up the driveway, and a woman got out of the car and walked up the sidewalk to him.

"What the hell did you do?" Debra asked. "Christian was in the middle of something and told me it sounded like an emergency. Where's Elizabeth and Grant?"

Brady stood up and grabbed his sister-in-law in a tight, desperate hug as the tears streamed down. Deb sighed and hugged him back. "Okay, calm down. I am sure you screwed up big time."

Brady pulled away. "I did, and I don't know if I'll be able to fix it."

Deb motioned to his bag and for him to start walking. Only when they were in the car and on the road, did she continue. "Christian said something about you and Trina. Does she have something to do with this?"

Brady nodded and rested his head on the back of the seat, closing his eyes. *I fucked up so bad, and now everyone will know.* "I screwed up. I screwed up big time." Brady came clean to Debra. How Trina came onto him in the garage and his kitchen. "I tried to stop things. She just... I just didn't try hard enough. God! I'm stupid, and now Elizabeth took Grant to her parent's, and I called Christian."

"Well, Brady, I love you, but you are a dumb ass. Did you

think Elizabeth wouldn't find out, and if she did, she'd be okay with things, like she was in college? When are you going to grow up? You're a dad and engaged... well, you were engaged... anyway, I hope she's okay. She loved you." Deb stopped talking, rolled her eyes, and shook her head. "You're an ass, Brady. I'm done talking to you."

Brady opened his eyes just a slit and glanced quickly at his sister-in-law. "Go ahead, Deb, now would be a great time to say what you think. What's holding you back?"

She gave him a smirk, and they drove on in silence.

Brady dumped his duffle bag on the bottom bunk in Ben's bedroom. He slumped down on the mattress, needing to take a break and breathe. Cars and dinosaurs were everywhere. Legos were on a table in a corner. *What the hell did I do? He laid back on the bed and placed his arms over his face. Deb's right. I am a dumb-ass! I finally had the girl I wanted. Elizabeth was mine, but better than I ever imagined. Maturity and motherhood made her more beautiful. And I didn't change a bit. Still a college kid. Still making stupid decisions.*

"Hey, Uncle Bwady!"

Brady smiled as Ben came flying through his bedroom door and into his uncle's arms. Brady squeezed this little bundle of energy and turned him upside down, planting kisses on his cheeks as Ben laughed and tried to escape.

"Uncle Bwady! Stop!"

Brady let him go, and Ben sat up on his lap. "Mommy said I shouldn't botha' you, but I'm not a botha,' so I came to say hi. Where's Aunt Elizabeth?"

Brady's smile was small. *I hope she'll still be your aunt one day, but I doubt that's going to happen now.*

Brady blew a big breath out. "Well, buddy, she went home to see her mom and dad really quick, so I thought I'd come visit you and your dad."

"And Mommy and William. Right, Uncle Bwady?"

"Of course. How could I forget them? So, is there anything to eat in this house? I'm starving." Ben gladly pulled Brady down the stairs and into the kitchen.

"Uncle Bwady is stawving. He needs food to eat, Mommy."

Debra and Christian were sitting at the table their heads close together, deep in conversation.

"Lucky for him, I already made him something." Deb took a plate out of the microwave and placed it in front of Brady. "You know what, Benny? Why don't you help me get your brother to bed, and brush your teeth, then we can get dessert for you men."

"Yay, dessert!" Ben jumped up and gave Brady a high-five and skipped out of the kitchen. Deb gave Christian a deep kiss on the lips and followed her son out of the room.

Christian watched his wife and son retreat, then grabbed two beers out of the fridge and sat down at the table. He stretched out and crossed his arms over his chest. A deep scowl covered his face. He raised his beer to his lips and took a deep drink.

Brady finally finished his dinner. He felt like the weight of the world was jumping up and down on his shoulders, and he was suddenly exhausted and spent. "Aren't you gonna say you told me so? Go ahead. I deserve it. I screwed up."

Christian nodded slowly and drank his beer. "Big time."

Brady put his beer down and stared across the table. "That's all you have to say. No words of wisdom, or brotherly advice? I could really use some."

"What do you want me to say? You had the girl you've wanted for years. You were engaged to her. You have an amazing son. Your life seemed just about perfect. So yeah, I do have something to say. What were you thinking? Why was it so hard for you to just tell Trina to leave you alone?"

Brady hung his head. He gripped his hair, and taking a fist full, yanked in frustration. "I don't know! I wasn't thinking. Like you said, I had what I always wanted and still, I wasn't happy. I needed more. Dad always said I never focused and never knew what I wanted. Dammit—he was right!" Brady stood up and slapped his hands on his thighs while he paced the kitchen.

Christian wrapped his hands around his beer bottle. "Dude. You need to relax. Getting all pissed won't make things better. You need to think about what you want—who you want." He made eye contact with his brother, tilted his head, and lifted his eyebrows. "So, Brady, who do you want?"

Brady stopped and held his brother's gaze, his eyes hard and focused. "You know who I want."

Christian pursed his lips. "I thought I knew who you wanted, but your behavior didn't follow your heart. I have no clue who or what you want, bro."

Brady rolled his eyes and felt his heartbeat escalate. "Dude! I want Elizabeth. I love her." Christian raised a brow.

He started pacing again. "I talked to Trina today and told her to stop texting me and that we aren't a thing. I told her we were a huge mistake, and I'm going to do whatever I can to make things right. I told her that Elizabeth's the one I've always wanted." Brady stopped to take a breath as emotions took over him. He leaned against the counter and focused on his breathing as he stared at the floor. It felt as if his heart was breaking into a thousand pieces. "Then she called Elizabeth and planned to have lunch with her. That's how this all started. Anyway…"

He intertwined his fingers to emphasize his words. "I love her, Christian. I need Elizabeth in my life." He shook his head as tears welled up in his eyes. The loss he felt made his stomach churn. "Do you think I totally screwed up?" The only other time he could remember feeling anywhere close to this empty, and this alone, was when graduation was getting closer, and Elizabeth decided they needed to go their own ways. He should have fought for her then, but he didn't. He didn't want to make the same mistake again.

Christian walked over and placed his hands on Brady's shoulders. "I don't know, dude. I just know you've loved her for so long, and I hope you didn't realize too late how much you really need her. Now you've got to let her know, no matter how much work it takes."

Brady nodded in agreement and fell apart when Christian pulled him in for a hug. He clung onto his older brother as the tears fell. He felt as if someone had taken his insides and tore them to pieces.

Chapter 23

The next morning came quickly—too quickly.

Elizabeth was exhausted, and her head hurt from crying most of the night. She stayed up late talking with her mom. Her mom promised to take care of Grant in the morning, so she could have as much time as she needed. She then called Jessica and gave her an update of the mess which was her life, and finally fell into a troubled sleep and found herself waking often with tears soaking her pillow.

The quietness of her parent's house as she went through her morning routine was driving Elizabeth crazy, and she couldn't keep her thoughts from straying to Brady—where he was and what he was doing—*who he was doing*. Sighing loudly, she wandered to her bookshelf, picked out a book and went outside and sat under the Weeping Willow tree in the corner of her parent's backyard. The long flowing branches of the willow would be a sanctuary, hiding her from prying eyes, and the weeping matched the feelings of her heart.

She was trying hard to concentrate on the words on the page but wasn't having any success.

"Hey, Elizabeth." Jacob was walking toward her.

"So much for the willow branches hiding me."

Jacob laughed and sat down in the grass. He leaned against her and nudged her shoulder with his. "Sorry. I don't think you understand the meaning of camouflage. If you want to hide, I suggest not wearing bright yellow next to brown bark and green grass and leaves. You sort of stand out."

The simple gesture of his shoulder touching hers, and his friendly words, made her insides brighten, and she gave him a small smile. She felt the tension that had built up inside her release.

"Where's Grant?"

Elizabeth didn't take her eyes off the cover of her book. "My mom took him shopping with her, so I could have some alone time." She placed her book on the grass and wrapped her bent knees in her arms, leaning her chin against them.

Jacob picked up her book, turning it over in his hands. "Whatcha reading?"

"Honestly, I have no idea. I couldn't concentrate on what the pages said." Elizabeth turned her face toward his, and she felt a familiar warmth fill her as she remembered the feeling of getting lost in his sky-blue eyes. She sighed deeply and leaned over, laying her head on his shoulder.

Jacob rested his head on hers, trying to console his friend. "I guess you haven't talked to Brady yet?"

Elizabeth peered up at him. "Why? What do you know?"

"Christian sent me a text. I called him, and we talked. He filled me in on what happened."

"Wow. Nothing can be kept a secret. I haven't talked to

Brady since I left. I have no idea where he is, and honestly, I don't think I want to know. If I think of it too much, I start feeling queasy." She closed her eyes, trying to drive away all the images her mind conjured of Brady in Trina's arms and him not missing her at all.

"That's why I came looking for you." He shrugged his shoulder so she would pick up her head. "Brady's at Christian's house. Deb picked him up after you left. He's been there ever since."

Elizabeth cocked her head to the side. "How do you know that?"

"How do you think? Christian told me. He wanted you to know where Brady was, so you wouldn't be thinking anything crazy."

Elizabeth looked Jacob in the eyes. "What, like he went running to Trina as soon as I left and has been fucking her ever since? Why would that ever cross my mind?" Because he seems to always run to her. He needs to grow the fuck up.

Jacob held back a grin, pinched his lips together, and took a big breath. "Look, you're hurting—and you should be. What he did was a jerk move, but in a way, it's a good thing he's at Christian's." Elizabeth raised her eyebrows and resituated herself on the grass.

"Okay," Jacob continued. "Well, Christian mentioned that Brady didn't want to be alone. He's been avoiding Trina's texts and felt that if he went home, she'd come to the house."

Elizabeth flinched. That's a mental picture she was trying to avoid. Jacob put his arm around her shoulder to comfort her.

"See that as a good thing."

"What? The fact he's admitting that he can't say no to her if she shows up and throws herself at him. That's supposed to make me feel good?" Elizabeth's voice started to rise with her racing pulse.

Jacob grabbed both of her arms and held them tight. "That's not what I mean." He paused, seeming to search for the right words. "I'm so sorry, Elizabeth. I just can't believe he hurt you like this. I really thought he cared for you."

Elizabeth fidgeted absently with the grass but lifted her eyes to meet Jacob's. He caught her gaze and held it. Her eyes studied his intently, and she felt her breath catch in her throat.

She and Jacob were so close together, she could smell his cologne. The scent took her back to a year ago… when he caught her attention… when they went on a bowling date… when she started to have feelings for him…when she was in his bed.

Her hazel eyes swept through his blue ones like they were trying to find something in the depth of the sea. She cupped his jaw, the stubble prickly under her palm. She pulled his face toward hers, and their lips met. His lips were warm and sweet, just like she remembered. Her heart pounded but there was something missing.

He backed away at about the same time, unlocking their lips. She felt him searching her eyes. "Elizabeth, we can't do this."

She closed her eyes, knowing deep in her soul he was right. She sank her chin to her chest before she peeked at him.

"We both love someone else." Jacob placed his hands on her

shoulders. His voice was light. "Right now, you and Brady are having problems, but you and I had our chance."

Elizabeth nodded, a smile growing in agreement, and turned her head. Kristen's eyes locked with hers and were wide with rage. Elizabeth's chest tightened as she realized she had betrayed a fragile friendship. She was no better than Trina.

She jumped to her feet. "Kristen, wait!"

Jacob turned and muffled a curse under his breath and took off across the yard.

"Kristen…" He turned her to face him. Her breath was rapid. She crossed her arms and shot him a cold, hard stare.

Elizabeth stepped around Jacob to meet Kristen face-to-face.

"Kristen, please. It was my fault." Elizabeth paused to catch her breath, holding up a hand. "Okay, I kissed him. It was stupid and meant nothing. I don't want to ruin what you two have. Truly, Kristen, he loves you." Elizabeth tried to make eye contact with her, but she kept turning away. "I'm so sorry. I know we aren't close, but we're trying to be friends, and I know first hand how shitty it is when a friend messes with the one you love. That was so wrong of me. I was being selfish. I didn't mean to hurt you."

"Whatever, Elizabeth." Kristen glared at her, shaking her head. Her eyes turned toward the sky, and she laughed harshly. "I've heard your relationship's in the shitter, and it seems that now you're trying to get back with my boyfriend but stay away. I don't need you starting to screw with us. Leave us alone."

Elizabeth glanced quickly at Jacob. He lightly squeezed her

arm, and she turned and headed back home.

Her day of relaxation and peace wasn't going quite as planned, so she headed to Jessica's to get the moral support of her best friend.

"Hey, you." Jessica gave her an enormous hug when she opened the door. "I'm so glad you came over."

Elizabeth returned the much-needed hug, resting her head on her friend's shoulder a little longer. She closed her eyes and breathed in a shaky breath.

"Hey, you good?" Jessica asked with concern in her voice.

Elizabeth pulled away and gave her friend a small smile. "Yeah, I am. It's just been a crappy day. A crappy past couple of days really."

They went into the kitchen and sat at the small counter. Elizabeth rested her head in her hands.

"So, what happened now?" Jessica asked. "Your text seemed concerning."

Elizabeth peered at Jessica over her arm. "I kissed Jacob. Kristen saw."

"Holy hell, woman! What's your problem?" Chad hollered as he entered the kitchen.

Both Jessica and Elizabeth jumped at his voice.

"Kissing Jacob while upset because your fiancé had a thing going with someone else. That is royally screwed up." He smacked his hand on his forehead and made a crazy grimace.

Both girls just stared at him for a second.

Elizabeth spoke in a quiet voice. "I guess I need to embrace when I make stupid decisions. She did tell me that just because my relationship... and I quote... 'is in the shitter'... she didn't want me to mess up hers. What the hell was I thinking? I'm no better than Trina."

Chad nodded. "Now that's taking things a bit far. You had a bad moment. Nothing came of it. Anyway, they'll be fine. We all know you're both over all that junk between you two."

Jessica looked at Chad. "Umm, this is supposed to be girl time."

"She's my friend, too. Her life's going to hell, and she just kissed my best friend. So, I think I can put some thoughts in on this as well."

Jessica rolled her eyes. "Well, I'm sorry, but you need to go. I can support my best friend just fine without your help."

"Well, her heart's been torn out, and she's depressed. What if it rubs off on you?"

Elizabeth watched them like she was watching a tennis match—her head swapping back and forth between them.

Jessica sighed and smiled. "Chad, now you're being ridiculous. Please, give us some time."

"Girl time, girl weekend...where does it end? How does it end?"

"It all ends with me in your arms and us wrapped together in your bed." Jessica stood on her tiptoes and laced her arms around his neck. "You, my handsome man, have nothing to worry about unless you've been cheating on me?" She smiled at him.

"I'm not crazy." He crushed his lips against hers.

"Okay, you two. You aren't alone, you know. Remember,

I'm the one whose life, is in the shitter." Elizabeth had to swallow against the tears that were coming to the surface.

Jessica placed her arm around Elizabeth's shoulder. "Sorry about that."

Chad turned so he could see both women. "Okay, now I need to get something off my chest."

Both girls lifted their eyes.

He glanced between them and breathed deeply before he spoke. "This is serious, girls," he said in a firm voice.

Jessica raised her eyebrows at Elizabeth, and they both busted out laughing.

"Anyway, I was driving through town and witnessed something. I don't know if I should say anything, but I think I need to."

Jessica hurried him on with her hands. "Well, what did you see?"

Chad braced himself on the counter. "Brady was with Trina at the park. They looked like they were in a serious conversation."

A groan escaped from Elizabeth. *I knew it. He can't stay away from her.* She leaned her head on Jessica's shoulder, glad she had someone's support.

Chad continued. "It didn't look like they were having a good time if that helps any. She looked angry and wasn't looking at him. He seemed to be needing her to pay attention... I don't really know and probably shouldn't have brought it up."

I'm tired of all this. My heart can't take it. Elizabeth pinched lips and wiped her hands through the air. "It doesn't matter.

You know what? I'm looking forward to this girl's weekend. I need this girl's weekend. Screw Brady and his immaturity."

"Yeah. Screw Brady and his immaturity." Jessica bumped Elizabeth's shoulder with hers.

Chad tilted his head back in laughter. "Elizabeth, you're a bad influence on my girl. He grabbed Jessica around the waist, dipping her. "I think I like it."

Jessica laughed and pulled him in for another kiss.

Elizabeth took a deep breath. "I need to go to the townhouse and get some of Grant's things and my clothes. I'm pretty sure Brady isn't there. At least Jacob told me he's staying at Christian's—trying to avoid Trina."

Jessica scrunched up her face. "How does Jacob know that?"

"Christian told him. Anyway..." Elizabeth took in another shaky breath and sat up straight. "I've gotta go pick up clothes, and toys and I would like you all to meet me there in a little bit to help carry out stuff. What do you say?"

"Please, like you have to ask. You're our friend. We're happy to help you." Jessica gave Elizabeth a hug.

Chapter 24

A couple hours later, Elizabeth felt her heart shatter into a million pieces as she stood in the doorway of her town home. Memories crashed into her like waves on a beach. Everywhere she looked, she saw Brady and her, happy, loving each other, laughing, holding Grant. But then, Brady's selfish choices wiped it all away. Her happiness. Her life with him. Her family.

"Are you good?" Jessica asked.

"Yes. I'm fine." Elizabeth took a deep breath, pulled her shoulders back, and climbed the stairs. Jessica and Chad followed closely behind.

With a bag in her hand, she went first into Grant's room, and placed as many clothes as she could into the duffle bag. She then stuffed his favorite stuffed animals in as well. She grabbed his crates of toys from his closet and items from the bathroom, and lugged all these out into the hallway, stacking them by the steps. Jessica and Chad took them to the car while Elizabeth entered her bedroom.

Adrenaline and hate took over as she stormed into her room.

How dare he do this to their family. She threw open their closet.

How dare he be so selfish. She slammed her suitcase on the bed.

How dare he treat her like trash. She flung her clothes into the suitcase.

Anger and betrayal fueled her. She wanted—no, needed—to get this finished and get out of this house. Out of Brady's life.

Suddenly, a hand dropped on her shoulder, and the familiar scent of wood and soap filled her senses. Her entire body stiffened, and her breath stopped. She dropped the armful of panties and bras she was holding, back into the drawer and gripped the edge to stabilize herself. Without seeing Brady, she knew it was him. She could sense him as if they were one person. His familiar scent surrounded her and crept into the cracks of her shattered heart. She closed her eyes to get her composure before she spoke.

"Get your hand off me," she spoke calmly through clenched teeth. "You have no right to be here."

"Elizabeth, please look at me." The desperation in Brady's voice tore through what was left of her broken heart. "Don't do this. I love you."

The last piece of calm and strength she had holding herself together, splintered when those words crept into her ears. She reared on him like a cobra going for the kill. Her pulse raced, and her body grew so hot, it was like a fire was spreading over her neck and face. Tears filled her eyes, but for now, the dam held.

"Don't you tell me that. Do not use those words!" She spit

venom at him as she pushed her hands against his chest—once, twice. Brady stumbled back just a step, his shoulders slumped, and his head fell forward, unable to look at her in the eyes.

"How dare you tell me you love me!" Her voice rose as she lost her composure, yet she no longer cared. "You promised me you wouldn't hurt me, but the entire time you were stabbing an invisible knife in my back. You chose to hurt me, Brady. You twisted that knife. You chose to hurt Grant."

Brady stood staring down at the carpet. He didn't deny what she said or try to fight it.

"Look at me when I'm talking to you!" Elizabeth screamed, and rage took over, filling her heart. She needed him to see the hurt he caused her. "You deserve to show me that courtesy."

He slowly looked up for a split second, and tears fell from his eyes.

Now you feel bad. You finally realize how much you screwed up.

For a second, she felt pity, until quickly her rational brain took over and squashed that emotion. The fractured pieces of her heart had no room for pity.

Whatever composure she had left evaporated in that second. She closed the gap between them and sent her hand careening across his face. The sound of her hand connecting with his cheek echoed in the otherwise quiet house, and the sound lingered in the air like the reverberating tone of a bell that had been rung for a final time.

"You have no right to cry, or to feel bad." She spat the words at him. "You knew what you were doing. You made the choice, and you did this to us. Your selfishness broke us!" Breathing hard, Elizabeth cradled her stinging hand in her arm, and took a step back. Exhausted. Spent.

Brady's eyes changed from sad and forlorn to seeing red. He squared his shoulders, and jutted out his chin, rubbing it slightly where it was slapped. "You know, I don't know why I came here hoping to pick up the pieces… to apologize. You are being so irrational." He ran his hands through his hair and breathed in a deep breath. He turned to walk away.

Elizabeth stepped around him and blocked his exit. "Excuse me? You're here to apologize? I'm being irrational?" The dam holding back an ocean of tears broke. She wiped at her face and her eyes pleaded. "Brady, it's like you never left college. Playing with people's hearts and feelings isn't a game. You made a commitment to me and Grant. You failed."

She stopped to breathe. She gently brushed her hands over his jawline where a red welt was starting to form. Her fingers slowly combed through his soft brown hair, through those waves she loved to touch for five years now. He wanted her and fought for her, only to throw it away. It didn't make sense. "Brady, why couldn't you just be happy with me?"

He reached up to wipe away the tears slowly falling down her cheeks. She closed her eyes, taking in the feeling of his touch on her skin. Her eyes blinked open, and she again gazed into his coffee brown eyes. The last piece of her shattered heart, which had been hanging on with hope, slowly fluttered down to earth with his silence. Calmness washed over her.

Elizabeth placed her hands on his chest, over his heart. She straightened up her slouching shoulders. "Brady, if this was really mine, you wouldn't have needed to go somewhere else. Like you said last year when you were in the hospital, if we were meant to be, we would have been a long time ago. Maybe that's what we knew in college. Maybe that's why our hearts never loved each other years ago. We have a baby, so Grant must be our connection for now. He's all we have left."

She removed her hands from his chest and crossed them over hers. Her once sad and broken heart now repaired itself with cement, and she felt a cold loathing for this man in front of her, and her voice came out calm and strong. Stronger than she realized she felt. "You made that choice for us. Now you have things the way you wanted. Leave. Jessica and Chad are here to help me. Jacob's on his way. Grant and I will be gone from your life in an hour."

She stepped to the side, giving him space. He stared at her and raised his hand to brush back a stray piece of hair and tucked it behind her ear. He leaned in as if to give her a kiss, but she backed away. He dropped his hand, left the room, and walked down the steps.

When Brady threw open the door, Chad and Jessica stood there. Brady jumped in surprise.

"Hey... Brady..." Chad moved out of Brady's path and glanced at Jessica pulling her lightly out of the way.

Brady gave them a small nod of recognition as he left his

house. He lost everything. His girl, his family, and his friends. A lump caught in his throat. As he walked down the sidewalk toward his car, his phone notified him of an incoming text.

"That better not be your slut you're texting while Elizabeth is still in your house."

Brady looked up from his phone as a car door slammed shut on the road. His eyes found Jacob's, and a stab of jealousy and disdain sliced through his already cracked and bleeding heart. Brady stiffened at the sight of Jacob standing in his driveway, walking toward Elizabeth, as he was being forced to leave her behind.

"Gonna step in and fix her now that she wouldn't forgive me and threw me out?" Brady felt his pulse race, and his nostrils flare as his breathing picked up. He was ready to confront Jacob with his fists if necessary.

Jacob stalked up the driveway with his hands clenched at his side, ready to do battle. "You really expected her to forgive you after how you treated her?"

Brady's phone pinged again.

Jacob motioned to the phone. "You better answer it, or you might be losing two girls in one night, then I guess you'll have to jack off to get what you want."

Brady glanced at his phone. His jaw clenched, and his blood boiled as he read Trina's text.

Trina: I know what you said earlier, but don't forget
I'm here if you need someone to lean on.

The embers of Brady's smoldering heart ignited and caused an explosion deep inside his chest so severe, he jumped and landed one punch across Jacob's face, catching him off guard. A crack, like the sound of splintering wood, filled the air. Brady landed another punch to Jacob's gut. Jacob caught his breath and jumped at Brady, landing a punch across his chin.

"Okay, dip shits. Enough!" Chad's enormous bulk jumped between the two men, anger thundering in his voice. "Killing each other is a great way to show a girl how much you care." Chad pushed them both back, keeping hold of Brady. "What the hell man? Remember who screwed up. Deal with your shit. You caused it." He pushed Brady away and kept his gaze locked on him.

Brady shook his hand. A pain shot through it where it contacted Jacob's face. He leaned over to get control of his ragged breathing and stared at the ground. He felt empty and alone, though he was standing with guys who he once considered friends.

"Dude, you okay?" Chad went to check on Jacob and was trying to get a good look at his face.

Jacob shook him off and stepped away with a scowl. "I'm good. I'm fuckin good." He wiped at the blood running into his mouth, wincing in pain when his hand brushed his nose. "I think this dick busted my nose."

With that, Jacob glared at Brady. His eyes bulged, and he lunged. His fist didn't fully connect with Brady's face, because Chad—once again—got in his way, keeping him from hitting his target full-force.

"What the hell's going on here?" Elizabeth rushed out the door and down the walkway, with Jessica following. She stopped. Her eyes wide as she took in the sight before her. Chad was holding back a pissed and bleeding Jacob. Brady was holding his face where he was just punched.

Elizabeth looked back and forth between the two guys. Seeing the blood on Jacob's face made her heart lurch. "Jacob, are you okay?" She reached out to touch him.

He flinched away from her hand. "I'm fine, Elizabeth." Their eyes met. "I promise. It's not as bad as it looks."

She pivoted quickly toward Brady. Her eyes shrunk into slits as she glared at him. She shook her head but kept her voice surprisingly calm. "Why are you still here? Get out of this driveway. Get the fuck out of my life."

Their eyes held on to each other's.

Brady moved forward, just briefly, and opened his mouth as if he had something he wanted to say. Then snapped it closed.

Finally, he got into his car and backed out of his driveway.

Chapter 25

Elizabeth heaved a heavy sigh fighting the instinct to run after him. Her heart, which she didn't think could break anymore, ached with a hurt so intense she started gasping for breath. Soon Brady's car disappeared around a curve and possibly from her life for good.

Jacob placed his hand on her back, breaking the silence and the tension surrounding them. "Elizabeth, I..."

"Shut up Jacob. Just shut the fuck up and go get cleaned up." *I can't deal with this right now.* Elizabeth turned and dashed back to the house. Jessica went with her, putting her arm around her friend's shoulders.

As soon as they crested the top of the staircase, Elizabeth stopped, and the weight of her night finally slammed into her. She turned to Jessica and fell apart. Tears poured down her face.

The wail that tore out of Elizabeth ripped through the walls of the town house.

"Oh, my gosh, Liz. I'm so sorry!" Jessica buried her best friend in a tight hug. She squeezed and held her, as if she could squeeze out some of the pain. Elizabeth's legs gave way, and together the two girls crumbled to the floor, but Jessica still would not let go of her friend.

The hug from Jessica helped. She was glad she had a forever friend. At least she had someone who was not going to let her down.

Jessica rocked Elizabeth as she cried. The tightness in her chest loosened, and soon her cries became sobs, then her sobs became hiccups.

Finally, she pulled away, peeled herself off the floor, and walked into the bathroom. She blew her nose and threw water on her face, trying to wash the night away, and the tears from her face. Jessica grabbed a towel from the rack, and without saying a word, handed it to her.

Elizabeth dried her face, looked in the mirror, and took a deep, cleansing breath. She made eye contact with Jessica in the mirror and gave her friend a small smile. Jessica rubbed her back and smiled back in the mirror. "Are you a little better?" she asked.

Elizabeth nodded. "You know, I could use a drink."

Jessica smiled. "Let's go down and get a glass of wine and check on Jacob and Chad."

The sun rose on a new day. Elizabeth planned to spend it organizing their things and getting them situated back in her parent's house. After she had a bite to eat, she loaded Grant into his stroller and headed out for a walk to help clear her head.

By the end of the walk she felt lighter and could breathe easier.

"Hey, Elizabeth. Hey... Oh, he's sleeping." Stacey met Elizabeth at the road as she was getting the mail out of her mailbox.

"Yeah. It seems that way. A stroller ride usually does get him drowsy. He's been up for a while. I guess he'll have an early nap. Would you like to come in and have a cup of tea or coffee? I really need to talk to you about something."

"Sure. I'd love that." She placed the mail back in the mailbox and followed. Elizabeth quirked her eyes. Stacey just swiped her hand through the air. "It was all junk. I'll let Jacob worry about it."

"Would you mind heating up some water, and go ahead and make yourself a cup of coffee. I'm gonna put him in his crib. I'll be right back." Elizabeth picked up Grant and ascended the steps while Stacey went into the kitchen.

Stacey sipped her coffee and peered at Elizabeth over the top of her mug. "You know, the first time I was in here was about this time last year. I came to check on you after you got sick at my house. I saw the abortion clinic on your laptop."

That was a nightmare which turned into a miracle. Elizabeth sighed. "That seems like a lifetime ago. So much has happened since then." She leaned over and picked up a framed picture of Grant her parents had on the table. She stared at his face and big brown eyes and felt warmth seep through her entire body.

Her face beamed as she gazed at the picture. "You know, it's so hard to imagine my life without this adorable little boy. I can't believe I almost chose a different path. He's changed my life, and I'm a better person because he's in it."

Stacey moved closer so she could see the picture better. "He's so cute. I absolutely love getting to know that little one. You made such a good choice. Honestly, last year, I didn't think having a baby was the best thing for you to do." Stacey stopped, glanced at Elizabeth, giving her a smile. "I'm so glad you made a more mature decision, than I think I would have."

A text on Elizabeth's phone interrupted their conversation. Trina. And she was coming over.

Now.

Elizabeth gripped her phone so hard her knuckles turned white.

"Liz, what's wrong?"

Elizabeth turned her phone to Stacey. "It's Trina. She wants to talk and is on her way over. What the hell can this bitch want now?"

There was a loud knock on the door. The girls looked at each other in surprise.

Shit. She's here.

Elizabeth got up from the couch and Stacey followed. Trina stood there with her hands on her hips and a scowl on her face.

"We need to talk." Trina pushed her way into the house, past Elizabeth and Stacey, and into the kitchen.

"Umm, excuse me, but I don't think you were invited in, Trina" Elizabeth followed and leaned against the counter, crossing her arms. "But now that you're here, what the fuck do you want?"

Trina glanced hard at Stacey, who stood next to Elizabeth. Stacey held her gaze and took a seat at the counter. Her chin on her fists.

Trina's eyes rolled skyward. "Look, I'm just letting you know you won. He's yours."

Is this bitch serious? Elizabeth did a quick shake of her head. "Wait, excuse me, I didn't know we were having a competition. What exactly are you talking about?"

"Brady." Trina's eyes rolled and she sighed. "He told me that we were finished. I didn't believe him at first, and after hearing about you leaving, I tried to comfort him, but he refused me. He said his goal is to get you back, and he has no time for me. He said it's always been you, and I was a mistake." Trina's eyes became clouded with hate and contempt. "So, I'm done here. I'm leaving, and you won."

She is serious and immature. She hasn't changed at all since college. Elizabeth raised her eyebrows and glanced at Trina, giving her a once over. She thought back to their first days in their dorm, the freshman activities they took part in, and the friendship she thought she had made.

Trina used to be fun and someone Elizabeth could trust. Maybe it was a false trust. A false friendship. She wasn't better, or prettier, or easier to like. She was always a snake. "You know what, Trina? I'm standing here thinking back over our college years. All those years, all that time we spent together. All the guys liked you—you were so outgoing. You were so pretty. But now, I realize you were just jealous of me. You made sure you were the center of attention. You made sure you were the one the guys noticed first."

Elizabeth stood, with their eyes locked, one hand on her hip, the other gesturing in the air. "You succeeded with all the guys but one. Brady didn't notice you first. You were always just a leftover. Someone he went to when I wasn't around. You were never happy that Brady and I had something more."

Elizabeth paused. Trina's eyes gleamed with tears. She pushed her chin up, but without the confidence it usually held. Her bottom lip was sucked in, her teeth on top. Elizabeth let out a breath, and in that moment, her sadness for Trina changed to pity.

"I didn't notice this when we were at college, but I understand it now. We didn't see relationships and feelings as real. They were just things to manipulate and play with. Sex was just sex. Nothing more. Getting pregnant made me grow up faster than I wanted to, and because of that, I've changed and grown since we graduated. I'm no longer playing a game. My love and relationship with Brady aren't a game to me, and I can tell you that if he still thinks it is, he's sadly mistaken." Her gaze passed to Stacey who gave her a smile and nod, encouraging her to continue.

Trina pressed her back against the counter and crossed her arms across her chest. "Are you done?"

Elizabeth took a deep breath. "No. I'm not."

Trina let out a heavy breath.

Elizabeth continued. "I've learned a lot of important life lessons this past year, but I think the most important thing I learned during my pregnancy and everything I've been through, is that no one can truly ever love me until I love myself. I hope that you understand that one day. You need to love yourself—not be in love with yourself—but love who you are and where you are in life. If you don't, no one else will ever be able to respect you—to love you. And we are meant to be loved, Trina. We truly are."

Trina's mouth hung open. Finally, she rolled her eyes toward the ceiling. "Whatever, just know I'm gone. I don't want him anymore or need him. He's all yours. Enjoy your life." Trina turned quickly and took a few steps, then paused but kept her back to Elizabeth and let out a loud breath. "He told me to make sure you know that he told you the truth. Yes, we've slept together since I've been here, but it was only that one time—not that I didn't try to get in his pants more than that—he is wrapped so tight around your finger, you cutting the cord will be the only way to get him loose." She pushed her head back and stalked through the front door.

Stacey looked at Elizabeth "Well, I guess I can say it now. I didn't like her. I thought she was a conniving bitch."

Elizabeth smiled. "Well, I learned that sometimes we have to be okay with moving on and leaving friendships behind."

"So, what are you gonna do about Brady?"

Elizabeth shook her head. "Nothing yet. But I need to talk to you about something that happened yesterday. Have you talked to Kristen?"

Stacey looked at Elizabeth as a small smile played on her lips. "If you're asking if I know about the kiss you and Jacob shared under the Weeping Willow, yeah, I heard about that."

Elizabeth scrunched up her face. "That was so stupid and talk about a big mistake. Anyway, the one thing good that came from it is that I realized I have no more feelings for your brother. I told Kristen that, but I don't know if she believed me. Do you think she did?"

Laughing, Stacey nodded. "Don't worry, I'm pretty sure Jacob convinced her."

Elizabeth breathed a sigh of relief. "Good. Then we have a girls' weekend to get started. I really need to get away for a bit and have some fun, and I need to pack."

"Yep, me too. It's time to spend Brady's money and make him pay—literally— for how he treated you. I guess I'll see you soon."

Elizabeth laughed and gave Stacey a hug, then went upstairs and took advantage of Grant sleeping and packed her bags.

Soon, all the girls were at her house. She gave her parents hugs, and Grant tons of kisses, and they all piled into Stacey's car, and headed toward the mountains of East Tennessee.

Chapter 26

The night was slightly cool, yet the fire in the fire pit was relaxing and consumed Brady's thoughts. He found himself alone on a Friday night with a beer in his hand, lost in self-pity as he watched the flames dance.

"Hey, Brady. Whatcha doin'?" Christian asked, as he, Chad, and Jacob sauntered into his backyard, their arms piled with food and beer.

"What're y'all doing here?" Brady asked. He watched as his backyard and quiet night was invaded. The guys dumped their goods on the table and filled the cooler Brady had next to him. Christian passed a beer to each guy and grabbed a piece of pizza from the box as he plopped down on a chair next to his brother.

Brady glared at Chad and Jacob. He didn't think they would talk with him ever again, especially not this quickly, anyway.

Christian slapped his hand on his little brother's back. "Bro, we're having an intervention." Brady froze, his beer bottle halfway to his lips and cocked an eye brow. "See, we could do a few things. One, let you mope all weekend wondering what the girls are up to. Two, you could make even stupider choices—which I don't think is something you would do since your life is crap right now. Or three, we could come and help you figure out your life while we all get sloshed.

Chad joined them around the pit and placed the pizza on a chair between them so they all could reach it easier. "Yeah, and we chose three. Our girls are out, thanks to your wallet, so we don't have anything else to do, anyway."

Brady glanced at Chad and his brother before he finally made eye contact with Jacob. *Chad makes sense. He's here because Jessica put him up to it. But Jacob? Why would he be here? We wanted to pulverize each other just a few days ago.* "What are you doing here? Enjoying the fact that I'm still without Elizabeth?"

Jacob sat down on the other side of the firepit and lifted his hands in surrender. "Look, dude, I'm on Elizabeth's side. I was just pulled here by these guys. I want to know what you were thinking and why you chose to hurt her."

Brady stared across the fire at the one who seemed to still hold a piece of Elizabeth's heart. He took a deep breath, finished off his beer, and opened another one taking a big gulp. "Last time I saw you, our fists did the talking. And you seem happy to step in to watch my boy when there's an emergency. It seems to me you're still a little too quick to jump in and be Elizabeth's knight in shining armor. Our fists don't need to work this 'intervention' out for us, do they?"

Jacob shook his head, looking down at the ground. "Why do you have to make this so damn difficult?" He glared across the fire at Brady. "Since you brought it up, let's remember why I had to look after Grant. Her parents couldn't. They needed to go to the hospital because you were too busy banging your side chick."

Brady shot him an icy glare.

Jacob held his gaze and continued. "Look, there's nothing left for us to work out. Elizabeth and I realized what we had is over."

Brady's icy gaze turned to fire. *Why does this jack ass always have something to add. He needs to leave Elizabeth alone.*

Jacob continued. "When she first moved home... after she left you... I saw her sitting under the willow tree reading. I went over to her to talk and be a friend."

Brady's stomach rolled, and he wondered where Jacob was going with this, but he held his gaze.

Jacob smirked and sat up taller. "At one point during our talk, she leaned over and kissed me."

Rage built up inside him. *Seriously! What the hell!* He launched out of his seat. Christian and Chad jumped up, prepared to stop him from jumping over the fire at Jacob, but Jacob stayed seated. He never flinched and didn't drop his gaze.

"Bro, let him finish. You need to hear what he has to say," Christian said as he placed his hand on Brady's arm, trying to calm him, yet also ready to grab him if he made the leap over the fire.

Brady turned on his brother with his eyes wide. "You knew about this and didn't say anything."

"Really? You have issues with this after what you did to her? Just wait. Listen." Christian held his hands up, begging him to relax.

Jacob continued. "The kiss went nowhere. I love Kristen. Now, that's a whole new discussion of drama, and could become a really good movie, but seriously. She's all I need, and Elizabeth knows her feelings for me are gone." Jacob held Brady's gaze. "... but now I see Elizabeth as more like a sister. I care about her. I love her, but I'm not in love with her. I promise." He glanced at Christian. "Now, I'm supposed to ask you for a truce, but what I want is to know you're going to work your ass off and prove to Elizabeth you made a huge mistake, and it won't happen again. You need to prove to her, and to us, that you'll be faithful. So, explain yourself."

Brady's shoulders fell. He did not doubt that he would be faithful—if he got a chance to. "I was stupid. There's nothing else to say, and I won't make an excuse. Trina came to my office and made a move. It just happened. Elizabeth told me I needed to grow up, it isn't college anymore. I know she's right. Right now, I lost her, and I need to work to gain her trust back. Hopefully, she'll want to start over." He paused and took a breath. "I also need to apologize to you. We started off on the wrong foot when I saw you and Elizabeth last year kissing in the parking lot. Being a friend to you has been difficult. I'm offering you a truce." He held out his hand toward Jacob. "Could we try to be friends?"

Jacob turned to Chad, who nodded, then he leaned across and shook Brady's hand. "Okay, dude. I hope what you said is true. Elizabeth deserves to be treated like a queen."

Brady collapsed into his seat and moved his gaze to the fire and popped open another beer. "I agree." *I don't know how, but I will do whatever it takes to gain her trust. I can't lose her.*

The flames danced and were hypnotizing. Brady looked around at the guys. "So, you mentioned something about an intervention and helping me figure out my life. I'm listening, as I have no clue how to fix this mess and get my fiancé and son back under this roof."

"Well, what have you tried so far?" Chad asked between a mouthful of pizza.

Brady sighed. "Well, I tried begging desperately for her not to leave and sort of apologized. And I yelled and called her irrational because the truth hurt. Then she kicked me out." He lifted his beer toward Jacob. "You know how well that turned out. I re-situated your nose."

"I don't know, it looks tough." Jacob touched his nose and raised his beer, taking a sip.

"And I had a couple night's sleep over with your son." He cocked his head toward Christian. "She won't return my calls or texts. I seriously think she's blocked my number." Looking at Chad, he continued. "You're engaged to her best friend. I'm sure you've heard something."

Chad hesitated, and focused on emptying his beer.

He shook his head. "Nothing that can help. She tried kissing him." He pointed at Jacob.

Jacob's eyes went wide.

Brady grimaced.

He held his hands up. "It didn't work, she realized she felt nothing for him. He's used property." Jacob threw a balled-up napkin toward Chad. Chad caught it and threw it into the fire.

"Seriously, you hurt her and broke her trust. She's tired of your immaturity."

Brady flinched.

"Sorry, man." Chad finished. "It's just what I know. But I think you might have a chance. I hope you're not against sending flowers and groveling. If you want her back, that's what you'll need to do. And if you screw up again, not only will you guarantee yourself to never get her back, but you'll have to fight Jacob and me. So, whatever you do, don't screw up."

Christian rubbed his face hard with his hands. "Look, Brady, I think you need to realize the level of the mistake you made."

Brady opened his mouth, but Christian put his hand up to stop him. "Wait... Think about it. How did you feel after you finally got together last year, and then you saw her kissing Jacob in the parking lot during your date?" Again, he held up his hand to stop the onslaught of his brother's defense.

This time, Jacob interrupted. "Dude, I'm trying to make amends here, and you're gonna bring up old wounds?"

Christian looked at Jacob. "Sorry, man, but there's a purpose to this." He turned back to Brady. "How did you feel when she came to see you when you were in the hospital?"

Brady stared into his beer bottle before he spoke. "I felt like my heart was torn out, and Elizabeth had trampled all over it. I didn't want to see her. I needed her to feel something real for me. I told her that at the hospital and asked her to leave."

Christian nodded. "And then she finally realized she loved

you. She gave her whole heart to you, and what did you do?"

Brady looked at his brother, and his view started getting blurry. Damn. "I fucked it up. Majorly. I had her and Grant. We were happy, but I couldn't make the right decision." Brady's heart was heavy. He was selfish. He messed up the one thing he wanted more than anything. He was thankful that Chad and Jacob were still here listening to him. He had a lot of fences to mend, and he hoped he could be successful.

"I know y'all are here because you care about Elizabeth and Grant. You want what's best for them. I promise each of you, if I can get her to talk to me again, and forgive me, I will be there for both of them and will put them first from now on. It might take a while, but I am determined to prove to her I love her and will be true to her. She makes me a better person. I need her in my life."

Now he just hoped he could get her back.

"Guys, the girls are out having fun, except yours, Christian, but here's to a girl-free weekend. We need to enjoy it. You know they are. They're hoping to get Elizabeth trashed and get her mind off..." Chad looked at Brady and saw panic flash through his eyes, "... Well, and with Stacey free, she's hoping to have some extra fun..." Seeing that didn't help Brady out at all, he stopped. "... Anyway..."

Chad shrugged and took a drink of his beer. "Do you think they'll have a pillow fight in bikinis?"

The guys all laughed.

Chapter 27

The girls walked through the door of their condo and into a large kitchen which had a great room open on to it. One entire wall of the great room was a large window looking out over the tops of trees, and a wraparound covered deck. There was a sliding door, which Stacey and Kristen immediately ran through to take in the view. It was astonishing. They were just out of town, and mountains surrounded them. The clouds were low and gave a smoky look to the peaks.

"We are so far above the trees. It's beautiful out here.... Oh, look. A hot tub and a bar!" Kristen poked her head back through the door into the kitchen where Elizabeth and Jessica were emptying bags of groceries. "I say we break in this hot tub and bar, get some food delivered by whoever delivers out here, and grab some drinks. The only thing missing is my boyfriend, but since we weren't allowed to bring him, I'll settle for extra alcohol."

Stacey pushed by Kristen and entered the house. "I agree with Kristen. Let's get this party started. Party here tonight and see what's happening in town tomorrow and party there tomorrow."

It didn't take long for the girls to put on their bikinis and get drinks in their hands. They stocked the outside bar with alcohol, mixers, wine, ice, and plenty of snacks. Once the food arrived, they dug into pizza and wings. Elizabeth filled shot glasses with tequila, passed them around with some limes, and had the salt ready.

"To a weekend without guys." She held her glass up high, impatiently waiting. Slowly, the others raised their glasses. "Really, y'all? You better be ready to have fun. I need to forget my life for a bit, and I need help. So, again, to a weekend without guys."

The other three raised their glasses, and they all took a shot and sucked the lime to help it down, shaking their bodies in the process. Stacey started to fill the shot glasses for a second round when Jessica's phone rang.

She dodged the shocked look from her friends and answered the FaceTime call as Chad's face filled her screen. "Hey, handsome."

The girls heard his voice answer her as Jessica walked around the edge of the house and out of earshot. "Where's she going?" Elizabeth asked as she downed another shot.

Jessica came back around the corner. "No, Jacob. She's not here. She got Elizabeth mad, so we dropped her off down on the strip and made her find her way back." Kristen shot Jessica a look as she walked to look in the phone. Elizabeth shook her head, and Stacey laughed.

"Hey, Jake." Kristen peered over Jessica's shoulder. "Where are you? Is that Br—" She stopped when she realized where he was, afraid to start an issue. "Why are y'all there?"

"Just hanging out and having our guys' night. So, what are y'all up to?"

Elizabeth and Stacey looked up, and Elizabeth drank down her third shot.

"Well, we just got in and are eating and enjoying the hot tub, but I'm not sure Elizabeth's gonna make it if she doesn't slow down her drinking. She's just took her third shot of tequila."

"Let her know we're keeping Brady occupied, in case she's interested."

She's not interested at all. Trying not to be anyway. If she gets her way, she will not have any worries all weekend.

Kristen answered Jacob. "Yeah, I don't think she cares at this moment. But we'll make sure she doesn't do anything too stupid. She's not the one I'm worried about. Your sister has plans you don't want to know about."

"Kristen!" Stacey shouted at her, splashing hot tub water at her friend. Kristen jumped back, squealing.

Jacob laughed into the phone. "Well, y'all take care of each other and have fun, but don't forget us guys back here waiting for you."

"You and Chad have nothing to worry about, Brady though, I'm not so sure."

The girls hung up and Elizabeth switched from liquor to beer.

"I'm sure you have Brady wondering what Elizabeth has planned this weekend, Kristen." Jessica said.

Kristen glanced at Elizabeth and noticed her roll her eyes. "Who cares? He needs to sweat and worry a bit about what

Elizabeth might do. He deserves any bit of panic and discomfort he has this weekend." Kristen held up an empty shot glass, and Elizabeth filled it with more tequila. The girls did another shot.

The night was going great. Elizabeth was feeling good, the hot tub was warm, the drinks were going down easily, the food they ordered was delicious, and the girls were having fun. "Okay, Kristen, time for you to come clean." Elizabeth looked at the girl she was determined to be friends with. "Now that you've had some drinks in your body, maybe we can talk heart to heart."

Kristen situated herself in a corner of the hot tub and lifted an eyebrow. "Go ahead. Try me."

Elizabeth smiled and took a drink of her beer. "Tell me why you didn't like me from that first night last year at Stacey's dinner party. What did I do that turned you against me before I even said hi?"

Kristen laughed and fell into Stacey. "That one's easy. You were sitting next to Jacob and had his attention."

"That's what I figured. But you realized, I had just met him. Like, that night."

"Yeah, but when you know him like I do, I could tell he was already into you. It was annoying. Just a few days before, he and I went to a movie, and made out. I thought we were going to finally be something more, then I walked in, and there you were, and he was all over you."

The girls became quiet. The only noises were the crickets, which sang an early song as the sun went down, and the soft whirring of the hot tub motor and the splash of the water from the jets. Stacey slapped her friend across the back. "Kristen, why didn't you tell me you and Jacob had gone on a date? I had no clue."

Kristen flinched away and laughed. "Ouch! Anyway, I didn't have a chance. You were working the night shift. I was bored. He called me and asked me to grab dinner and a movie." Kristen looked off into the distance. "It was a great night. We really talked for the first time in a long time, laughed, and enjoyed each other. It was never like that before. There was no alcohol involved. There was nothing either of us was running away from. It was just two people enjoying each other. I thought it was going to be different."

She sighed before she continued. "Even his kisses were different. Usually they were just kisses, but these seemed..." She hesitated and looked off in the distance, thinking. "... More intense. He even looked at me differently, like he really saw me for once. Then just two days later, I walked in—he was looking at you, and it was just like things were back to what they used to be between us."

Elizabeth felt awful. It was almost like she got in between the two of them. "Kristen, I'm so sorry. If I would've known..."

Kristen shook her head. "It doesn't matter. It all worked out. It was like it took you and him not working out for Jacob to finally realize that he had feelings for me. He liked me in high school. I used him then. I liked him after high school. He used me then. Now we both want to be with each other. We don't need anything."

She looked sadly at Elizabeth. "You know, Elizabeth, I'm really sorry for being so bitchy to you over the past year. I mean, I tend to be a bitch on a good day, but I was ultra-bitchy to you, and for no reason except for jealousy." Kristen stopped and a smile passed between the two girls. Maybe they could become friends. Their dislike has been a big misunderstanding.

Stacey looked at her best friend and leaned over, engulfing her in a hug. "Kris, that is such a sweet thing for you to say." She rocked her back and forth. "My brother must have softened that rock you have in your heart."

Laughing, Elizabeth jumped into the hot tub and splashed through to the other side. She wrapped Kristen in a hug. "Apology accepted!"

Kristen looked at Elizabeth and smiled.

Jessica and Stacey were laughing, and both jumped in the tub with the other two.

The girls splashed each other. Kristen tried to block the sprays of water with her arms and climbed out of the water. "Okay. Enough already. I'm glad you all think my words are so funny and worth a laugh. See if I apologize anymore."

Elizabeth climbed out after Kristen and squeezed her shoulders. "I just want you to know I'm glad you came this weekend, and if I would've known there was something between you and Jacob, I would never have pursued him. But it all seemed to work out. You're with Jacob, and I'm with… well…" Whatever. It is what it is.

Elizabeth sighed and shrugged. She grabbed the shot glasses and tequila bottle. She filled up four shot glasses with tequila.

"One more shot. Here's to new friendships and confusing relationships."

Kristen flashed her a smile. "That I can drink to." All the girls clinked their glasses together and drank down their shots, shaking their bodies to help the warm drink go down.

Loud country music and awful singing woke Elizabeth the next morning. "What the hell? Turn down the music!" she yelled from her bed and as she did, the motion of yelling and rolling over simultaneously made her head start throbbing and her stomach churn. She grabbed the cool pillow beside her and placed it over her face. The temperature of the pillow felt good against the pounding of her head.

"Wake up, sleeping beauty. I have something that might help you." The pillow muffled Stacey's voice and floated off her face. Elizabeth's eyes opened slightly. Stacey sat on the edge of the bed with a pill bottle in one hand and a five-hour energy in the other. "Here you go. A little bit of vitamins to help your hangover and some pills to soothe the headache. You and Kristen need to get moving. We have shopping to do, food to eat, and a party to find. You better be feeling up to it soon."

Elizabeth gave Stacey a death stare as she downed the pills with the energy shot.

"Good, that's better. Now go hop in the shower, and Jessica and I will have breakfast and strong coffee waiting for you as soon as you get out."

Elizabeth rolled her eyes but got out of bed and jumped into the shower. She made sure the water was scalding as she got in and wished it would wash away her headache.

As Elizabeth was sitting eating breakfast and drinking her third cup of coffee, she video called her mom to see what her parents and her son were up to today.

Her mom picked up on the first ring. "Hey, you!"

"Hi, Mom." Elizabeth tried to smile, but it came out sort of like a grimace.

Her mom laughed at her through the phone screen. "Well, it looks like someone had a little fun last night." Her dad's voice and his deep laugh echoed from across the kitchen. Her mother walked toward him.

"Good morning, Lilly-Billy. Look who's here." He held up Grant so she could see his little face in the camera.

Elizabeth's heart lifted and her lips turned up. "Hey there, little guy. Can you see Mommy?" Grant laughed into the phone, but of course they couldn't tell if it was because he saw her or it was something else.

"So, what are your plans today?"

Her mom sat in the chair by her dad and Elizabeth could see her place her arm around the boys. It was so sweet. Her mom and dad, and Grant. She took a screenshot of them.

"Well, we thought we'd head into town. There's going to be a little festival in the park. It's gonna be a nice day. And…"

"What's going on, you two? What aren't you telling me?" Elizabeth's words became sharp.

Her dad answered. "Well, Brady called last night and asked

to see Grant. We told him to meet us there and he can have Grant for the rest of the day. He wants to take him to his parent's house."

She may not want to see him, but at least he hasn't forgotten about Grant. She forced a smile on her lips. "That's fine. Grant is his son."

Her dad handed Grant off to her mom; his face grew serious. "Elizabeth, I know Brady messed up. I'm not happy with him. He knows he messed up." Elizabeth sighed and looked away from the camera toward the ceiling.

"Hey, don't roll your eyes. Just look at me." She smiled a large sarcastic smile at her dad. "That's better, Lilly-Billy. Anyway, Brady came over yesterday, and he and I had a talk."

What! Why can't Brady just stay away? He chose this. "Dad, really? Why?" Her voice went up a notch as she interrupted her father.

"Why? Because he asked to, and he loves you. He wants to make things right. Trust me, he has a lot to prove. He broke my trust when he broke your heart, but I still think what you two had is worth it. You both light up when the other's around. Sometimes people screw up when relationships are new, unfortunately it happens, but people can be redeemed." He paused and took a deep breath. "I'd like you to listen to him when you get back. Think about what I said, that's all I ask. Now I gotta go, and I'm sure you girls have big plans. I'll see you tomorrow when you get home."

She smiled at her father. Her mom put Grant back in his arms, and Grant put his hand on his grandfather's face. The smile they shared melted Elizabeth's heart. She pushed the buttons to get another screenshot.

She smiled at the camera as her dad placed a kiss on Grant's cheek. "Dad, I wish I could just find a man as awesome as you, and a love as amazing as your love for Mom and us."

Jackson smiled back. "I know, honey. And as your dad, I've prayed for a man to love you. Someone who is strong enough to admit when he is wrong and someone who will love you through the good times and the tough. I want you to have the love your mom and I do. And I know you can."

Again, Elizabeth sighed. "Okay. I'll think about talking with him. Thank you so much for always being there for me. I love you."

"I love you too, Lilly-Billy."

Jessica and Stacey poked their heads into the phone screen. "Bye Mr. Parks. We love you." They both said together.

Elizabeth and her dad hung up. Her dad's laughter still lingered in her memory.

"Now that everyone got their phone calls out of the way, and we've all eaten, let's get out the door and get this day started." Stacey corralled the girls, and they headed out the door.

Chapter 28

After a busy day of shopping, sightseeing, and hiking, the girls were tired and hot. They quickly strolled back to their car to throw in their bags and found a restaurant with a dance floor and bar, just off the strip.

"Wow! I'm starving." Stacey dropped down into a chair at a round table and grabbed the menu. Soon, the server placed a basket of rolls and waters in front of them and took their order. The girls dove into the basket like animals who hadn't eaten all winter as they waited for their food.

Soon, all their plates were scraped cleaned, and more margaritas were ordered; Elizabeth noticed Stacey was not really paying attention to what they were talking about and glanced behind her to see what was taking up all the girls' attention. Elizabeth's eyes fell on a table with two handsome men. One had dark hair, the other light brown hair. They had fine chiseled features and both filled out their shirts nicely.

She elbowed Kristen and gestured with her head behind her.

Kristen glanced quickly and turned back to her friends, nodding. "Stace, what's got your attention?" Kristen asked as she looked at her friend and followed her eyes again across the restaurant.

Jessica looked and raised her eyebrows.

Kristen turned her head at once. "Well, Stace, that's a good-looking table. Very easy on the eyes. Which one have you've been watching?"

Stacey laughed, pink crept up her neck, and she emptied her drink in one gulp. "Enough, y'all. Stop staring." The guys were leaning in, talking intently. "Great. I think they noticed you gawking at them."

"Us?" Kristen said with an incredulous look on her face. She motioned around the table. "It doesn't seem that we were the ones gawking. That was you, little girl." She said this in the tone Kristen usually got when trying to play the 'I'm taller than you' card.

"Shit." Stacey cursed under her breath, as Jessica started to blush. She picked up the drink menu, pretending to read it.

"What's going on?" Elizabeth turned toward the sound of a chair being pulled over. She briefly made eye contact with a guy with dark brown hair who sat beside her. While his friend sat down next to Stacey, his chair turned backward.

"Hi there, ladies." The handsome Adonis next to Elizabeth greeted them.

Elizabeth couldn't take her eyes off the size of his biceps. He had short sleeves with cuffs so tight it looked like they were cutting off his circulation. She could make out a part of a tattoo of an eagle on his arm. She moved her eyes off his tattoo and massive arm and up to his face. Here she melted into deep brown eyes. She cleared her throat and took a drink.

He looked at her and smiled a wide toothy grin. "My friend

and I noticed that y'all looked like you were having a lot of fun, and we felt left out. I hope you don't mind if we join you?" He smiled at Elizabeth, then turned to Jessica, then Kristen. "I'm Adler, and this here is Tristan." He motioned to his friend sitting across the table.

Tristan's eyes were locked on Stacey's and he stuck his hand out toward her. "Tristan. Nice to meet you."

Stacey smiled at him, not removing her eyes from his. "Stacey." She placed her hand in his, and instead of shaking it, like everyone expected, he raised her knuckles to his lips and brushed a soft kiss on them. "Glad to finally meet you, Stacey." His voice came out soft, yet husky, with a slight southern drawl. Stacey smiled in return.

"Tristan, you're as old-fashioned as your name, aren't you?" Kristen took a drink of her margarita. "And Adler, that's unique."

Adler smiled at Kristen showing a mouthful of perfect teeth. "Adler means, eagle, and like the eagle, I'm laser focused and can see what I want from miles away." He winked at Elizabeth.

She held his gaze until her insides burned, and she had to turn away and gasp for breath. A smile turned the corner of her lips up. "Hmm, miles away, or just across a restaurant?"

"Either one. Does it matter?" His eyes dug themselves into Elizabeth so deep she wasn't sure if they would ever be able to find their way out.

Jessica placed her elbows on the table and leaned her chin on them. "Well, Adler, tell us something about yourself? Are you guys from around here, or are you like us and just visiting?"

"We're just in for the weekend. We live west, near Nashville. How about y'all?"

The conversation continued and the girls found out that the guys didn't live far from them. It was a small world. Soon, another round of drinks found their way to the table, a band started playing, and people started filling a make-shift dance floor.

Tristan smiled at Stacey and cocked his head toward the dance floor. "Would you like to dance?"

"I'd love to." Stacey gave him a sly smile and mischief glinted in her eyes. "Come on, y'all. Join us." She pulled on Kristen's hand and drug her on to the dance floor behind her. Kristen motioned for Elizabeth and Jessica to follow.

Jessica shrugged. "Why not!"

She grabbed Elizabeth's hand, and Adler followed. Soon they were all on the dance floor, laughing and dancing. The Electric Slide came on, and the girls talked the guys in to staying, and they easily followed along to the steps.

Tristan pulled Stacey into his arms as the music slowed. Kristen gave her a thumbs up and winked, as she and Jessica left to grab a seat at the bar and ordered a drink.

"Stay and dance with me." Adler gently grabbed Elizabeth's hand.

Guilt flooded her. *Get over it. It's just a dance. Not like you'll do anything. You're not Brady.* She nodded and he wrapped his arms around her. She placed her hands lightly on his shoulders and looked up into his eyes. This close, his smoky gray eyes looked almost dark—like storm clouds.

Adler leaned into Elizabeth's ear. "So, tell me about that ring on your finger. Who's the lucky guy?"

Elizabeth looked at the diamond shining in the light of the dance floor, and that familiar knot formed again in her chest. "Well, that would be my fiancé." She breathed in a shaky breath and blew it out slowly. "Honestly, I forgot I had it on. He and I haven't been getting along lately. He made a stupid mistake, and I don't know what I'm gonna do."

Adler lifted her left hand off his shoulder and glanced at the diamond as he moved it around her finger. "Well, any guy willing to do something stupid, and let you go, isn't in their right mind."

Elizabeth looked up at him. He wasn't quite a head taller than her, but those eyes! "You have amazing eyes, Adler. They belong with your name."

"Yeah, they do their job to get me the attention of a beautiful woman."

Elizabeth laughed at him and felt the intenseness of his gaze. She knew she should go, she should walk away, but she felt drawn to him. "So, tell me what you do." They had to yell into each other's ears to hear over the music and noise of the crowd, but Elizabeth felt more relaxed talking or yelling, than just looking into those eyes.

His smile bore a hole through her. "I'm an accountant for a firm. How about you?" He leaned back just a bit. If Elizabeth wasn't careful, their lips would easily collide.

"Honestly?" she asked with a bit of a flirtatious tone.

He tilted his head and gave her a smirk, showing off an

adorable dimple in his left cheek. "I'm a web designer for small businesses..." She hesitated, wondering how much more to tell him. "... and a mom to the most adorable little guy you've ever seen."

He fanned the fingers of her left hand out on his. "I'm gonna guess that this ring was given to you by the most adorable little guy's father." He raised his eyebrows.

Elizabeth stopped dancing. And looked at her finger, then up at the man in front of her. "Yeah, but like I said, he made some poor decisions, and to be honest, I don't know if I'll be able to forgive and forget." *Adler is...Wow. But can I just let Brady go?* Her heart was thumping wildly. Anticipation, or nerves?

Finally, Adler broke the silence. "I'm a little warm. Want to get a drink and some fresh air?"

Elizabeth nodded, and Adler pulled her off the dance floor and ordered two drinks at the outdoor bar, where surprisingly there weren't many people. They walked to a railing where they could sit down their glasses and admire the lights in the small town.

"You know, if you were my girl, I wouldn't make any poor decisions." Adler ran his finger down the length of her arm. Elizabeth felt her heart do a leap or a thump. She wasn't sure, but she knew that he was a lot closer than he probably should have been, but with all the alcohol in her, she didn't really care.

She glanced sideways at him and gave him a little smile with a twist of her head. "Yeah, well, too bad I'm not yours. You could teach Brady a thing or two about how to treat his girl."

"Brady, huh. Well, Brady's crazy. You're too beautiful to be here dancing with another guy."

Elizabeth turned her head completely toward Adler a little too quickly. Their lips were just inches from each other. She stared into his eyes and felt the heat and desire of his gaze penetrate deep into her soul.

He reached out, lightly touching her cheek with his hand, and leaned slightly closer to her. Elizabeth could feel the touch of his breath on her skin. She pictured what it would be like with his lips on hers. Why did this man send chills down her spine when she's still in love with someone else? You're better than that. Don't be like Brady and Trina. She held her breath as guilt suddenly washed over her. She saw brown eyes in her mind—Grant. She lowered her gaze and took a step back.

"Umm, Elizabeth. We're ready to go." Jessica said from the entrance of the patio.

Elizabeth put one finger up so Jessica would wait, and her eyes met Adler's once again. "I'm sorry. I need to go."

He gave her a small smile and pulled a business card out of his pocket.

"Here. In case things with Brady don't work out. I'd love to see you again." He smiled at her, squeezed her hand, and walked away.

She watched him go and the knot in her stomach loosened. Kristen and Jessica both watched his retreat before turning back to her. Elizabeth leaned on the railing and watched the action of people and cars filling the street. She swished the ice around in the glass, not really interested in the watered-down drink.

Jessica placed an arm around Elizabeth's shoulder. "So?"

Elizabeth just shook her head and sighed "Am I crazy for still loving Brady?"

Jessica squeezed her friend tight, "No, you're not. You have a history and a son." Elizabeth dropped her head onto Jessica's shoulder.

The girls stood there, looking out at the view before them. "This is beautiful," Jessica exclaimed. "I can see why people love coming to the mountains."

"Yeah, the view isn't bad." Kristen agreed. "Especially when its name is Adler." All three girls laughed.

Stacey walked out on the patio. "Hey, I wasn't sure where y'all went."

Kristen turned and smiled a wide smile. "So, where's Tristan? It seems like you two were having a good time."

Stacey's shoulders came to her ears. "Yeah, we were. Did you know that they live close to us? Looks like I just might see him again." Joy lit up her face. "Maybe one day I'll find that guy. Now that you and my brother are happy, it's time for me to put myself really out there."

Kristen looked at her best friend. "What's that mean? Are you saying you haven't focused on any of your guy friends because you were too busy playing mom to Jacob and me?"

Stacey nodded. "Yeah, well, someone had to put you both first. You sure didn't. That was a full-time job."

Jessica gave Kristen a hip bump. "Yeah, especially when Kristen tended to become a handful and rude to everyone around her. It was a full-time job for you, Stacey." Daggers shot from Kristen's eyes. "There's that look I'm used to seeing." Jessica laughed.

Kristen rolled her eyes. "Whatever."

The girls laughed and decided to head back to the condo and continue the party there.

Chapter 29

Early the next morning, the girls were tearing through the hotel room, a little hungover from their late night, trying to get packed, and out of the condo before they got charged a late fee.

Elizabeth heard her phone ringing. "Someone find my phone, please."

"Here, I found it." Kristen grabbed Elizabeth's phone from the edge of the hot tub. "It's Jacob." She yelled to Elizabeth and answered. "Hi, Jake," she cooed. "Why are you calling Elizabeth?" She walked back through the house and found Elizabeth in her room.

"Kris, I need to talk to her. It's an emergency." Jacob pleaded.

Kristen looked at Elizabeth. "Here, it's Jacob. He says it's an emergency." Kristen about threw the phone at Elizabeth.

Elizabeth went into panic-mom mode. Her eyes became enormous, and her heartbeat picked up its pace as she grabbed the phone from Kristen and pressed speaker. "Jacob, what's wrong? Is Grant, okay?"

"Grant's fine. He's here with me. It's your dad." Jacob paused, and Elizabeth's heart leaped. "Your dad's had a heart attack."

Elizabeth fell hard onto the bed, the phone shaking in her hand. Fear filled her from head to toe, and she couldn't move. What could be wrong? She just talked to her dad yesterday. He seemed fine.

"Elizabeth." Jessica kneeled beside her, took the phone from her shaking hand. "Jacob? Elizabeth's in shock or something. What's wrong? What did you say to her?"

"She needs to get to the hospital. Her dad had a heart attack. I have the baby. Jess, it's pretty serious."

Her blood drained from her face, and she stared at Elizabeth. "Okay. Okay. We'll take her straight there. Unfortunately, it'll take a while. Keep us informed." She turned to Elizabeth and squeezed her hand. "Liz, it's gonna be okay. We'll take you to the hospital."

Elizabeth was frantic by the time Stacey reached the hospital. Her eyes were red, and her leg hadn't been still the entire drive.

"Everything's gonna be okay." Stacey pulled up to the main door of the emergency room, then turned around, laying her hand on her friend's knee. "Let us know how things are going. We're going to go help Jacob with Grant." She made eye contact with Jessica, and Jessica nodded.

Elizabeth took a in a deep breath to calm herself. She closed her eyes and said a silent prayer. Slowly opening her eyes, she gazed blankly at the Emergency Room entrance in front of her.

A lump formed in her throat and fear strangled her. Jessica put out her hand, which Elizabeth gratefully clasped and pulled herself from the backseat.

Jessica led Elizabeth through the Emergency Room doors. Worry and concern covered Elizabeth's face and she had to force her legs to move forward. She stopped in her tracks when she saw Brady sitting with her mom and was thankful that Jessica was there to pull her on.

"Mrs. Parks." Jessica called softly across the almost empty waiting room.

Charlotte, who had her face buried in her hands, glanced quickly toward the voice.

Her mom's face was crumpled and tired. Her eyes were red and swollen from crying. Elizabeth picked up her pace and engulfed her mom in a hard, desperate hug. They both cried a river of tears.

Elizabeth gained a little composure and pulled slightly away wiping her face. "Dad..." she couldn't finish her question and left it dangling in the air between them. She couldn't ask. She didn't want to know, not yet.

Charlotte shook her head and breathed in a shaky breath. "We don't know anything yet. I rode in the ambulance. They didn't want me to drive. Brady met me here, but I don't know anything. Your dad was fine. We were eating... then he just started having a hard time breathing... Then..." She fell again into Elizabeth's arms. Brady helped them to a seat.

Elizabeth just glared at him.

Jessica laid her hand on Elizabeth's shoulder. "Hey, I'm

gonna go call Chad and let him know where I am." She gave Charlotte a hug.

Brady spoke up. "I called him when I was on my way over here. He was going to help Jacob."

Jessica smiled at Brady. "Thanks, Brady. I'm gonna go call him, anyway." Her words were short, and she held his eyes for a second before walking away.

He let out a sigh and dropped into an empty chair.

Elizabeth held her mom close. What will her mom do without her dad by her side. They are a team. *God, please let him be all right. She needs him. I need him. Grant needs him.* She kept taking deep breaths to fight back the tears.

Time stopped as they waited. The low ringing of the phones. The sneeze of another man also waiting on his own news were the only sounds. The stench of bleach and bandages, and the scent of Brady's cologne were the only smells which registered in her nostrils. She covered her nose with her shirt, trying to keep both smells from her brain. They sent nervous butterflies into her stomach and hurt her heart.

She focused on her breathing as they waited and kept her eyes on her mom's lap where the distraught woman continued to nervously wring her hands. Elizabeth grasped them, giving her a comforting squeeze and laid her head on her shoulder.

Charlotte sighed and placed a kiss on Elizabeth's hair. "Thank you, honey."

"Of course, Mom." She answered without looking up.

Suddenly, Elizabeth felt the presence of someone sitting next to her, and again, Brady's cologne announced him. He offered her a box of tissues, which she took from his hands.

She cleared her throat, having to cough to make her voice work. "Thanks." Her voice was soft, but her eyes were not as they looked into his.

"You're welcome." He gave her a small smile, one you could miss if you weren't close to his face, and she turned away.

Finally, a doctor came out and walked slowly toward them.

Brady quickly jumped up to greet him, and Elizabeth helped her mother up.

The doctor's eyes were filled with compassion, and Elizabeth reached over to hold her mom.

"Doctor?" Charlotte choked out the word.

"Mrs. Parks, your husband suffered a heart attack. We tried everything to restart his heart, but we were unsuccessful. I'm sorry, but your husband has passed away."

Charlotte's eyes became wide and glassed over as she fell into her seat. Sobs tore from her chest. Elizabeth's stared blankly at the doctor. Brady touched her shoulder, but she flinched away from him, and dropped into the seat next to her mom. She pulled her close, and let her cry while Elizabeth held back the tears.

Her eyes closed. Her dad was gone. The man who held her little family together. The man who gave her a love of football and nature. The man who smiled with Grant on the phone just one morning ago. The man who demonstrated everyday what true love looked like by how he treated her mother, and his family was gone. Tears finally spilled from her eyes, and she pulled her mother closer.

Their pastor, and Charlotte's best friend showed up. They prayed together and talked with the woman.

Brady approached Elizabeth. He needed to comfort her, even though he knew she didn't want it from him.

He laid a hand on her shoulder, and she turned to him, her face was filled with grief. Her gaze tore into him.

Seeing her like this, this sad, this torn apart—again—broke him.

He pulled her in for a hug with apprehension, but she fell against his shoulder and clawed at him in anguish, tears streaming down her face, and cries tearing from her lungs. Brady led her into a chair and held her tight as she cried in his chest. "Baby, I am so sorry." He laid one hand in her hair and rocked her, placing a kiss on her head. His lips lingered there. If he could take her hurt away, he would. He closed his eyes as tears fell from them and Elizabeth wailed with distress.

Brady felt the presence of others and looked up to see Jessica and Chad standing over them. Jessica's hands were over her face, and Chad turned her to him.

Chapter 30

The next few days drug on as Elizabeth and her mother's lives were turned upside down. The man who led them, and was their anchor was gone, and at times Elizabeth felt like their ship was going down. If it wasn't for the support and love of their friends, their church family, and a little boy who needed his mother's love and attention, it would have been easy to just slip under that sinking ship and not come up for air.

Elizabeth did everything on auto-pilot. Focusing on her mother kept her busy and gave her a purpose. Her mother felt lost without her husband of over thirty years, and Elizabeth did all she could to help around the house and get ready for her father's funeral. Their friends came out in masses to show their support, deliver casseroles, and spend time with them.

Brady and his family helped out by taking care of Grant, so Elizabeth and her mom could have time to focus on what needed to be done.

With everyone's help, the funeral came and went, and soon it had been a week since her father's death, and Elizabeth needed to get back to her life. She was going back to work today and planned to pick up Grant at Brady's afterward. Elizabeth felt as if she had been in a dream all week.

Elizabeth woke early, wanting to get a walk in before work. She needed to clear her head and concentrate on the new life she had been given. A life without her dad, her rock.

As she walked around the neighborhood, her mind wandered to Brady and how helpful he had been lately. He was there for her and her mom without being asked. He brought them groceries, fixed dinner, cleaned the house, and did random jobs which her dad would have done. He kept Grant most nights, and his parents watched him during the day so she could help her mom tie up loose ends.

Even though Brady let her know he loved her daily, he took the cold shoulder she gave him, and the short responses. He tried to hug her once after the hospital, but she pulled away from him, her stare blank. Since that time, he gave her the space she needed, while letting her know he was there.

Her last conversation with her dad popped into her mind. Her walk turned into a jog. Remembering it was just the day before he died, brought tears to her eyes.

Her pace became faster as she tried to outrun the tears. *If I only knew, I would've said so much more.* She shook her head, to shake away the tears, and ran faster. She ran until she was gasping for air, then slowed her pace to catch her breath.

The promise she made to him flashed into her mind. She could see her dad's face on her phone screen as clearly as it was that Saturday morning. She promised him she would listen to Brady, that she would give him a chance.

She stopped walking and placed her hands on her waist breathing deeply and exhaling while she focused on the grass beneath her feet. She knew she needed to talk to Brady. Tonight, when she picked up Grant would be perfect, although she didn't know what to say.

When she got home, she flipped through the pictures on her phone and found the last one she snapped of her dad. The first morning of their girls' weekend. She looked at the man there with the smile as he watched his grandson, then she swiped sideways and saw the picture of Grant and her mom with him. They were all beaming at the screen. Elizabeth instantly uploaded them both to the drugstore's picture developer and ordered four pictures of each.

Elizabeth walked into the boutique and found Leila already going through the opening routine. Elizabeth made her way to the back room. Today was a day to work on the online store, get out orders, and restock items they found themselves out of again. Going through the receipts filled her with a feeling of pride. The online presence had been a bigger success than anything she or Barbara Stanzel could imagine. In just the few short months since its launch, the online store had made as much as the brick-and-mortar location. Elizabeth took the numbers to Barbara to show her how successful it was.

Barbara was speechless. Her eyes shone. "You've done an amazing job. I never would have been able to get that started. I'm so proud of you." She beamed at Elizabeth, and leaned back on the desk, crossing her arms. "I had dinner last night with some of the owners of the businesses in town. A couple of them would love for you to help them with their websites and get their online stores set up. This might be a business venture for you."

Really? Elizabeth raised her eyebrows and her mouth dropped open. Growing a small business through an online presence was what her plan was after graduation and here she was accomplishing her dreams.

Barbara nodded.

"Wow, that would be awesome! My own business."

During the day her mind kept busy with the work in front of her, and occasionally wandered to the possibilities of a web-store creation business. When her workday was completed, she checked in with her mom before heading to Brady's to pick up Grant.

Pulling into the driveway, she felt a mixture of emotions. She needed to cuddle her son and give kisses all over him, but this was the first time she had been back here since she left Brady. Her heart was battling with itself. She felt torn between her need to see her son and her nervousness about being inside the walls of the townhouse again. So much had happened since the night he drove away. Her heart was broken, her trust was crushed, but her brain still thought of Brady.

Her thoughts went back to the girls' weekend, and Adler.

How good it felt to be in his arms and look into his amazing eyes. How her insides heated. But now, thinking of him there was nothing, no feelings. Just emptiness. She had an out, someone who liked her and would spend the time to get to know her and Grant. Stacey was seeing Tristan and let her know Adler asked about her. But she wasn't interested. Her heart belonged to Brady, she just needed to figure out if it could be healed.

She stepped out of the car, and her eyes fell on the rose bushes they planted. She pulled off a yellow petal and felt the smoothness between her fingers. The day they planted these was a great day. Her heart skipped as she remembered the love they shared, and the happiness she felt. Just a couple days later was when Trina showed up and everything changed.

Elizabeth strolled up the sidewalk, absently caressing the rose petal. When she reached the door, her hand hesitated over the knob. She paused, trying to decide if she should knock or just walk in. "Get a grip, Elizabeth. You've never knocked before." She took a deep breath. The door opened easier than she anticipated, and she almost fell onto the floor. Fortunately, Brady was there to catch her.

"Hey, sorry. I thought I heard someone at the door. I guess I pulled while you pushed." He smiled at her as he held tight to her hips. She felt a heat deep within her body at his touch, yet she avoided his eyes and found herself staring at his shirtless chest.

Elizabeth composed herself and regained her footing. She placed her hands on his chest and her heart skipped a beat. She looked up slowly and found his brown eyes focused on hers. Her face flushed, and the small, unsure smile on Brady's face grew wider. His hands moved to her face and softly rubbed along her chin while the other curled a piece of her hair around its finger.

"How are you doing?" Brady didn't let her go, and his gaze burrowed into her eyes, burning a hole right through her.

Elizabeth's breathing slowed and she nodded. "I'm good. Mom's good. I'm looking forward to seeing my boy." She unraveled herself from his grasp and wandered into the living room. "Where is he?"

Brady gestured toward the playpen, and when she gazed in, she saw Grant asleep cuddled with his teddy bear in his arms, and his binky in his mouth. A smile crept across her face. She wanted to lean in and touch him but resisted. She didn't want to wake him.

"He looks like he's grown so much, and it's only been a week." She glanced at Brady with a smile.

"I know. When you don't see him, the little changes seem huge. It hurts to miss even the little things." Brady flashed his handsome crooked smile, which always dug into Elizabeth's heart.

She turned toward him and searched his face, wanting to feel sorry for him, but found she still held contempt and anger. "I'm sorry you missed so much, Brady, but you brought it on yourself. You chose selfishness over your family. Selfishness doesn't deserve happiness."

Brady's face fell, and his shoulders dropped. He turned from

Elizabeth, walking away from Grant. "Elizabeth, I messed up, and I know I can't expect you to forgive me so easily."

She followed behind him and felt her heart leap a little at the sadness in his voice. She reached out a hand to touch him but quickly pulled it back. Her insides playing a tug of war with her feelings. One side wanting to hold him, and take him back, the other wanting him to hurt more and worse; just like she did.

"I know you and Trina are over. She came to my mom and dad's house..." She paused as she realized what she said. Tears threatened to spill over at the mention of her father. Brady stepped toward her, but she waved him off and took a deep breath. "Anyway, she came over and told me what you told her. That y'all were through and you didn't want her. She said you told her you never wanted her. It was always me."

Elizabeth stopped and forced her eyes to make contact with the brown pools of his. "The problem is... the thing I have a hard time with, is that you told me the same thing— that it was always me. You also told my parents that, right in the kitchen when you first met them. But Brady, you went to her. You kissed her. You slept with her."

Her composure shattered as the tears fell and her insides shook. "Why, Brady? Why couldn't I make you happy? Why couldn't what we had satisfy you?"

Brady looked at the shattered woman in front of him. He shook his head and trailed his hands through his hair, pulling slightly, grimacing. "God, Liz. I wish I could understand why I did what I did." He looked at her. Her eyes were red, and tears soaked her face.

He shook his head and put his empty hands out and shook his head. "I don't know. I needed to grow up. I needed to realize what was important."

He stepped forward to engulf her in his arms, but she stepped back, hurt and sadness crossed her face. He stopped and wrapped his arms around his chest instead. "I know I have a lot to prove to you, and I am willing to fight for you as long as it takes."

He stood taller and squared his shoulders. He reached out and gently lifted her chin up, forcing her to look at him. His eyes pleaded with hers. "I was stupid, Liz. I made a huge mistake. I know that, and I know you have every right to leave me and never look back. I also know my words don't mean much anymore. I waited for your heart to love me, and then when I finally had it, I tore it to pieces. It was so wrong of me. I hope you give me the chance to prove myself to you. Do you think you can give me another chance?" He released her chin and lowered his hands to her wrists.

Elizabeth was at a loss for words. Her insides were all jumbled up, and her heart was beating so hard, she thought he could hear it. She looked past him; her gaze falling on a picture behind his head. A picture of the three of them, smiling, happy. Her heart fluttered. When she spoke next, her voice was small, tired, and she didn't make eye contact. "Brady, I want to believe you. I really do." She turned her face up to look at him. "But first, there's something I need to let you know."

She put a little space between them. "When we were in the mountains, on our girls' weekend, we had a blast. There were a couple of guys flirting with us." She stopped and looked at Brady. She felt defiance fill her body, and it gave her courage. "He asked me to dance, and I did. We danced a couple dances, fast and slow, eventually we went outside to get some air. We talked. He was a really nice guy." She stopped and focused on his face. "He leaned in to kiss me." She saw a flicker of frustration in his eyes, and his features tightened.

She smirked at his reaction and pushed her shoulders back. "How's that make you feel?" She studied him more and he continued to tense up. "It doesn't feel good, does it?" She walked away from him as she felt her voice start to get louder.

She grabbed the back of the kitchen stool, took a deep breath, and spun toward him with vengeance in her eyes and held his gaze. "I pulled away. I didn't kiss him. I thought of you and of us. I couldn't do it." Tears sprang to her eyes, and she wiped them away. "I hope you realize what you're feeling right now is nothing compared to what you put me through. I wanted to kiss him. But deep brown eyes stopped me."

Brady blinked back the tears.

Elizabeth gave him a smirk and her voice rose. "Oh, Brady. Don't give yourself too much credit. It wasn't your brown eyes that stopped me, but Grant's. I'm a mom now, and everything I do will reflect on what kind of mother I am, and I didn't want to let my little guy down."

She held Brady's gaze until he looked away. She could see the guilt in his eyes and her pulse picked up. She couldn't believe the hurt. She loved him with all she was. He threw it all away. She was going to explode. And she did.

She grunted through her teeth and her fingernails dug into the material on the stool. "God, Brady! Why did you have to do this? Honesty—you could've just been honest about your and Trina's relationship last summer. You could've come clean and told me you kissed her." Daggers shot from her eyes as they contacted his. He stepped back. "You could have refused her!" She hollered.

She reached up and rubbed her eyes, trying to control her rage. "I don't know what to do, Brady. I don't know."

Elizabeth went over to the playpen and gently picked up her still sleeping son with his teddy bear. He awakened a little, and she cuddled him into her arms, bouncing him gently, and breathing in his baby scent. She kissed him lightly on his brown curls. Her pulse relaxed and her breathing slowed.

She turned, and Brady was there next to her. "Liz, I know sorry's not enough, but I'll prove to you how I feel." He reached out and touched the ringlet that lay over her shoulder.

Elizabeth looked up into his brown eyes. Her voice was calm. "We are your family, Brady. We need to be your first choice. Everything you do will be reflected in this little one." She wanted to say more, but she felt tired and worn out.

She sighed before she continued. "Thank you for stepping in and taking care of him this week. And helping us. My mom really appreciated everything. Maybe you can come by next weekend." She held his gaze for a little more; there were no feelings apparent on her face. Then she turned and walked away.

She felt Brady walk up behind her as she opened the door.

He touched her gently on her back. "Elizabeth, can I see you both this week for dinner sometime?"

She stopped but didn't turn around. She nodded her head. "Yeah, I think so. Call me." And she walked out the door.

Chapter 31

The girls went for pizza after church on Wednesday night. Elizabeth, Stacey, Jessica, and Kristen sat around a table with pepperoni pizza and garlic knots between them.

"Okay, Elizabeth. You've been extra quiet tonight. What's going on?" Kristen asked.

Elizabeth just shook her head and kept her eyes on her pizza. Kristen stared her down.

Kristen laughed, and Elizabeth rolled her eyes. "Fine. Look, I've been thinking a lot about Brady. He wants to see us this weekend. I'm torn." She made eye contact with each girl. "The Saturday morning we were at the mountains, I Facetimed home and talked to my parents." She paused, breathing through tears which welled up in her eyes.

Her friends gave her the time she needed, and she finally gained her composure. "My dad told me he talked to Brady. He wanted me to give him a chance. He felt we could work things out. My issue, though, is that he cheated on me and Grant. We were living in his house, and he cheated on me. How can I trust him? I know my dad wanted me to, and I know he thought Brady deserved a second chance, but what do you guys think? Should I trust him?" She started picking the pepperoni off her pizza and tearing it to pieces as she waited.

Her friends just looked blankly at her.

She picked up a napkin and wiped her greasy fingers. Balled it up and threw it on her plate. "I don't know what to do, or what would be best for Grant."

Jessica sighed and took a sip of her Coke. "Look, it's ultimately got to be your choice. Can you forgive him? Can you trust him again? Do you love him? Is your relationship worth fighting for? We can't answer any of these questions for you. But we will support you no matter what."

Elizabeth's dropped her chin in her hands. "What do you think, Stacey?"

Stacey looked around the table with a smirk. "Look, I'm the only one never able to keep a relationship. But if you want to know, I think you should do what your heart tells you."

Unfortunately, they are right. It's her decision. No one else can make it. What does her heart say?

"I need to go home." Seeing the beginnings of objections from her friends, she waved them off. "No, it's early enough that I can still spend some time with my mom and help her get Grant to bed. Good night, y'all."

She smiled at her friends and walked away.

She quietly entered her house in case Grant was already asleep but heard her mom singing to him. She tiptoed to the sunroom, not wanting to interrupt. Her mom had Grant laying on her lap, and he was smiling at her, as she sang a song that Elizabeth remembered from her childhood. It brought back memories of her dad rocking her; it was the song he used to sing to her.

She leaned against the doorjamb and listened, a smile covered her face, and tears filled her eyes. When her mom finished, Elizabeth clapped. "That was awesome, Mom. I forgot about that song." She sat down next to her, and Grant turned when he heard his mother's voice. He leaned to her, so she took her son and cuddled him close.

"He was getting a little fussy, so I started telling him stories about his grandfather and that song came to mind." Tears fell silently down Charlotte's face.

Elizabeth adjusted Grant and placed her free arm around her mom's shoulders, laying her head there. "He liked it, Mom. He was just staring at you as you sang."

"Lizzy, I'm so glad the two of you are here. It helps me get through the tough days. Well, they're all tough, but it helps to know I'm not here in this house alone. Oh, I almost forgot. Those came for you today." Her mom gestured behind them toward the kitchen counter, by the coffee pot. "I put them there, so you'd be sure to see them."

Elizabeth stood up with Grant in her arms and walked to the bouquet of spring cut flowers in a vase. Daisies, Gerber daisies, and lilies of white, yellow, orange, and red were in a vase with greenery and baby's breath.

"They're beautiful." Elizabeth responded breathlessly as she reached for the card. Her heart started beating hard. She recognized Brady's handwriting.

This wasn't the first bouquet of flowers she had received from him. She remembered the ones he used to send to her before his fraternity formals. He would invite her that way, with a note inside the flowers. He knew these were her favorite.

Her mom came over and took Grant from her arms. "Here, honey. I'll take him to bed. I'll be right back." Elizabeth kissed Grant on the cheek and watched her mom walk with him out of the kitchen. When she heard her footsteps on the floor above her, she opened the envelope, which was square like a large card.

Elizabeth gave a big sigh and read:

Elizabeth,

Our gardens are filled with your flowers. Whenever I walk outside, or in the backyard, they're there, and I think of you. They brighten my day and give me something to remember you by. I know I screwed up, and all the words in the world will not make it right. I want to prove myself to you, and hope you give me the chance. Please meet me tomorrow—I know it's only going to be Thursday, and I asked to meet you this weekend, but I have more I want to say, and I need to tell you in person. Your mom already told me you have the day off, so please meet me at noon.

Forever,

Brady

Elizabeth stared at the card, turning it over and over in her hands. She took an internal evaluation of her feelings and noticed that she didn't feel tears or sadness. She felt hollow, tired, and empty.

Her feelings for Brady had been all over the place the past few years. If she wouldn't have been pregnant, they probably wouldn't have talked. But she had gotten pregnant, and they did talk again. The familiar butterflies started in her stomach again. It was hard to deny her feelings for him. This time after her dad's death would have been so much harder if Brady wasn't here for them.

She looked up as her mom returned to the kitchen. "He went right to sleep. He's such a good little boy." She smiled and placed her hand on Elizabeth's shoulder. "Those are really thoughtful."

Elizabeth looked into her mom's eyes. "Should I forgive him, Mom? The last conversation I had with Dad, he said I should. I don't know, though. Would that make me weak? Would people think I need a man?"

Her mom kept quiet as she turned on the kettle and got mugs out and tea bags, never turning around.

Elizabeth stared at the flowers. He was trying. The flowers are beautiful. She continued flipping the card over and over in her hands.

With two mugs of hot water and tea bags, her mom joined her again at the counter.

Elizabeth smiled in thanks and started dunking her tea bag in and out of the water. "Mom, is it too much to want a love like you and Dad? You two were always in love. You were perfect."

Laughing, Mrs. Parks sat down on the stool next to Elizabeth. "Lizzy, your dad and I didn't start out as amazing as you think. Our first few months of dating were hard." Her mom covered Elizabeth's hand with hers. "When we met, he was in a relationship, and he had a hard time ending it, even though I thought he did."

Elizabeth's eyes got wide. "What—he cheated on his girlfriend with you?"

Her mom nodded. "Yes, but he told me he broke up with her, but he was dating us both for a while, until he got caught."

"Wow, Dad!" Elizabeth's brow creased with worry. "It all worked out, though, right? He chose you."

"Yes, eventually, but first I walked away and wanted nothing to do with him. You see, I fell hard and fast, and I thought he felt the same way. When I found out he was still seeing this other girl on the side, I was hurt. When I walked away from him, it opened his eyes, and he fought to get me back."

Charlotte combed her fingers through her daughter's hair, and Elizabeth leaned into her mom's hand.

Charlotte placed her fingers on Elizabeth's chin. "That's why your dad talked with Brady. He wanted to see how sincere the boy was. That's why he told you what he did on the phone. He felt Brady knew the extent of the mistake he made and really wants to work things out." She stopped and caught her daughter's gaze, making Elizabeth's heart beat a little faster. "I know how it feels when your heart's been torn out and trampled by someone you thought loved you. I wouldn't say this if I didn't feel it's true because my instinct is to guard you from all hurt, but he does love you, Lizzy. You can see it in how he looks at you and talks about you."

Elizabeth swallowed down the lump forming in her throat and looked at the flowers. She thought of their relationship, and their life with their son. The happiness they shared. The hurt he caused. Her heart skipped a beat, and angry tears welled up in her eyes. "Mom, I understand what you're saying, but Brady and me aren't you and Dad. We have a son. We were engaged — are engaged—what if people think I'm weak getting back with him." She stopped and buried her face in her hands.

Her mom gently pulled her hands away. "Hey, look at me." Elizabeth turned toward her mom.

"It doesn't matter what people think. Haven't you figured that out by now? It's about you. What do you think? What do you need to make you happy? Who do you want? If love was easy, everyone would be in love, and no one would ever get divorced. Love's not easy; it's hard work. From the first day of your relationship until your last day of a thirty-year marriage. It's work. The only thing that makes that hard work easier is when the two people working together love and respect each other. That's what your dad and I did, and that's all we want for you. Someone who will love and respect you, now and forever. You and Brady might have started off rocky, but at least you know now, how hard you will each work to keep your relationship together. He's willing to work hard, and he isn't too tough to admit he was wrong. Those are noble traits in anyone."

She smiled at Elizabeth, placing a kiss on her cheek, and holding her gaze. "I hope you think about what I said, and what your dad told you. But I want you to know, whatever you decide, I'm on your side. If in your heart you feel Brady's just not the one, and you can't trust him, I'm with you. You know you and Grant are welcome here as long as necessary. This house is too big for one person. Even if you want to give Brady another chance, don't feel like you need to move back in with him. This is your home. Do you understand?"

Elizabeth smiled. "Yes, Mom. Thank you for everything."

"Of course. Goodnight, honey. I love you."

"Love you too, Mom."

Elizabeth sat in the kitchen a little while longer, drinking her tea and just staring at the flowers. *We never really had a real relationship. We never really dated. We went to fraternity parties, that's it. Maybe we should start over.* She finished her tea and went up to bed.

Chapter 32

Her nerves were causing chaos with the bagel she ate for breakfast, and the closer she got to her—his—their—(she wasn't sure what to call it anymore)—townhouse, the worse they became.

When she pulled up into the driveway, she took a deep breath, and her nerves kicked into high gear making it difficult to stay in the driveway. She gave herself a pep-talk. "You've got this, Elizabeth. Hear what he has to say. Stay calm."

She took another deep breath, and was ready to open her car door, when the garage door started opening, setting off another set of nervous butterflies.

Brady stood before her, and her heart skipped a beat.

He looked good. He was dressed in a pair of well-worn jeans and a basic gold T-shirt. His hair was getting longer again, and was a little messy, which she always found endearing, and a little—okay, a lot—sexy. He gave her his crooked, unsure smile, which always melted her heart, and she noticed it slowed down the crazy fluttering going on inside her.

"You got this girl." She climbed out of her car and walked toward him.

He gave her a once over as she approached. "Hi. I'm glad you came. You look amazing."

She smiled shyly at him. "Thanks—for the flowers."

Brady nodded and reached out and tucked her hair behind her ear. Elizabeth looked up at him. His eyes were red, and they looked like he had had a hard night, or maybe even been crying.

He ran his hand down her arm, causing goose bumps to form on her skin, and stopped at her hand. "Can I hold your hand?"

She tilted her head and grabbed his hand. He sighed at her touch.

"Elizabeth, I'm not gonna make excuses. I've already tried. I need you to know something. I love you. So much. But I want to ask you something, and I hope you'll hear me out." He paused. His eyes were desperate and pleading, and she felt him shaking slightly. She squeezed his hands. Hoping to reassure him, wanting him to continue.

"You and I have never had a proper relationship. At college we were together when it was convenient for one of us, for four years, but only spent a little more than one month exclusive. Now, because of Grant, we have just sort of been thrown back into something."

He drew in a shaky breath.

"I want us to start over, to date each other and do things right." He started to fidget with the engagement ring still on her finger, and a smile crept slowly across his lips. He held up her hand. "I'm surprised you're still wearing this."

Elizabeth glanced at her finger. "Honestly, I considered taking it off plenty of times. But just never did."

"I'd like you to take it off, now."

Confusion that passed across her face. *After all we've been through, he wants it off?* She raised her brows.

He held her hand tighter as he saw the confusion cross her face. "We jumped into things, a relationship, an engagement. If we're starting over and dating, being engaged needs to come later. I want to prove to you how much I love you. I know I need to gain your trust back. I'm willing to do whatever we need for us to be together, and I hope, when the time is right, this will come back. And if not, I hope you'll be happy. That's all I want. Your happiness."

Elizabeth took off the ring and handed it to him. She felt relief from deep inside her and her heart relaxed as if the cement she placed there to protect it had disappeared. "Last night, I was in the kitchen thinking and thought the same thing." She stood tall. "Starting from the beginning is exactly what we need. Just because there's a baby, doesn't mean we need to rush into anything, and honestly, I need some extra time."

"I know, and I want to give it to you. All the time you need."

She searched his eyes, and the glint of love she saw in them lit up her soul. "Thank you. Promise me you won't lose the ring, and I'll get it back."

His smile became wide, and he placed the ring in his pocket, then gently pulled her to him. "If you want it back, if you want me, I promise you it's yours."

Elizabeth placed her hands gently on his chest and felt the familiar warmth seep through her skin. This time, though, she didn't pull away. Instead, she stepped closer and slid her hand up to his face, brushing against the couple days' worth of stubble. When her eyes met his, she felt herself melting once again in those chocolate brown eyes. He leaned closer, then hesitated. Her heart—which had been cold and heavy for so long— skipped a beat, and she felt heat grow deep in her chest.

Finally, as their eyes bore into each other, her lips closed the gap between them and brushed gently against his warm lips. She closed her eyes, and found herself lost in his touch, his breath, his taste. It was a short, sweet, light kiss.

When they separated, their foreheads touched. Elizabeth kept her eyes closed and concentrated on all things Brady, the feel of his body under her hand, the feel of his hands on her hips and back, the smell of his cologne, the warmth of his breath.

Her eyes fluttered open and made contact with his. Her voice was soft. "Brady, I think starting over is a good thing, and I hope we can make us work out this time. You broke my heart and my trust, but I know they can both be repaired. My heart feels better already."

He lifted his hand to brush back her hair. He closed his eyes tight before then opened them slowly. "Elizabeth, thank you for giving me a chance."

Her eyes filled with tears. "Brady, I need your promise. I need to know and feel that I am enough for you, for now and forever." Her heart, which had been broken, was now mostly repaired but needed this one last promise.

He shook his head slowly. "I'll never forget how I hurt you and broke your trust. Sorry doesn't even come close to how I feel. I promise to show you every day and prove to you that you are enough for me forever."

Her eyes searched his, and her heart filled with happiness. A smile spread across her lips. "I'd love to date you. To start over."

A smile spread across his face, and he let out a heavy breath. "Thank you so much. I'll work every day to be worthy of your love." He stared into her eyes, making her butterflies return.

His hands found their way into her hair, behind her neck. "Thank you for giving me another chance. I was scared you wouldn't." His words were cut off as his voice cracked with emotion.

Elizabeth connected her lips to his once again.

Chapter 33

"Something smells amazing in here." Elizabeth was busy making pancakes and sausages when Charlotte entered the kitchen the next morning. Grant was already in his highchair enjoying his breakfast. She gave him a peck on his head, and he greeted his grandma with a big grin and a squeal of delight which caused pancake filled drool to come out of his mouth. She smiled as she made her way to the coffee pot.

Elizabeth placed pancakes and sausages on a plate and sat at the table. Her mom joined her. "How'd things go last night? I didn't hear you come in." Charlotte raised an eyebrow as she took a bite of her pancake.

Elizabeth gave a sly smile. "I didn't get in till late, or I guess you could say early." Her face lit up when she thought back to last night. "And we didn't do anything. Just laid in bed talking and holding each other." She looked up from her pancakes, toward her mom. "We're starting over. We've never really dated, just did…" she shrugged, "…well, you know. Anyway, we're going to date and see where things go. Take things slow. We're young and have a lifetime."

Charlotte nodded and her eyes gleamed. "That's a great decision. I guess you and Grant are here for a while then?"

"Yes. This is our home."

"I'm glad to hear it. So, what are your plans today?" Charlotte got up from the table and refilled her coffee.

"Brady's coming to get us and we're just going to take Grant to the park and whatever else we decide." She started wiping crumbs from Grant's hands and face. "Do you need me to help you with anything today?"

"Nope, I'm going out with some of the ladies from church. Shopping, a movie, and dinner."

The doorbell rang and Charlotte went to answer it as Elizabeth finished cleaning up Grant and set him on the floor. He crawled over to a basket of toys and started pulling them out.

"Good morning, champ."

Elizabeth's heart fluttered at the sound of Brady's voice behind her. She turned as he wrapped his arms around her waist.

"And, good morning, beautiful." Brady kissed her cheek before turning her to face him.

"Good morning." Her whole face glowed. As he leaned down to press his lips against hers, a warmth again spread through her body, and she fell against him. "Well, are you ready to go?" He laughed and messed with her ponytail held high on her head. She was still wearing the clothes she came home in.

"Yeah, no. You're early."

"I couldn't wait to see you. I'll spend some guy time with this little one while you get ready." Brady sat on the floor with Grant, and started building a tower with the big Legos his son threw all around him. "It's never too early to understand the principles of engineering."

Elizabeth laughed. "Well, that will make my morning easier, but he needs a bath."

He glanced up and gave her thumbs up. "Bath. Got it."

She could tell when she wasn't needed, so she turned and headed upstairs to hop in the shower.

The summer changed to fall, and Elizabeth's heart healed. Brady made her feel special and loved every day, even the days they didn't see each other were filled with time on the phone and talking. They learned things about each other they never knew before. Brady had never been out west and wanted to see the desert. Elizabeth feared heights. That one floored him. He had known her for six years and never realized she had a fear of heights. Brady hated salads. He liked lettuce on burgers but hated lettuce in a bowl. That one caught Elizabeth off guard, and she always laughed when she thought of it. She didn't like fish of any kind. Brady promised to change that.

Everything between them was new and exciting.

Jessica said it seemed like they were more comfortable with each other; Stacey agreed. Being with Brady this time was different. Elizabeth felt as though they really knew each other and were closer than they ever had been.

They were together now because they wanted to be with each other. Not because of sex. Not because of a baby. She loved him with her whole heart and soul, and he felt the same way.

It was late one night in early November when Brady brought Elizabeth home. They had been at Chad and Jessica's. "Hey, can we sit a minute?"

Elizabeth nodded and followed him to the porch swing. They sat and Elizabeth laid her head on his shoulder. She let out a sigh and closed her eyes. She could fall asleep here on the swing, leaning on him, and be comfortable all night wrapped in his arms.

Brady pushed the swing gently for a bit with his feet before he finally broke into the quiet of the night, combing his fingers through her hair. "I love you." He kissed her temple.

The feeling of his lips on her face and his fingers on her scalp was relaxing. "I love you, too," she whispered.

Brady moved just enough to cause her to sit up slowly and nudged her, so she turned toward him. "I want you to know, I never forget how close I was to losing you, to losing this." He stared into her eyes and brushed her cheek with his fingers.

Elizabeth smiled and her stomach gave that familiar flutter. She opened her mouth to talk, but Brady placed his fingers over her lips, stopping her words. He shook his head. "Let me finish, please."

Breathing deeply, he continued. "I need you, Elizabeth. I always thought I did, but now I know it. You make my life full, and me whole in a way I never thought possible. You're my best friend, the one that makes everything better and the one I want to share everything with." He paused and reached into his pocket.

He pulled out the ring that was once on her finger.

Elizabeth looked at it, remembering his words when she took it off. Her gaze moved to his and locked there. A smile filled her face, and she closed her hand over his.

"I promised you I'd keep this and give it back to you one day. I would love it if today was that day. I love you more now than I ever thought possible."

A lone tear fell down her cheek, and he brushed it away.

"Elizabeth, I promised you that I would show you and prove to you that you are enough for me forever. I hope that we can start our life together now, and I hope you know that you are enough. You are my everything. For now, and forever." He stopped and took a big breath.

Elizabeth's heart was beating out of her chest. Tears filled her eyes. When their eyes met, she was so filled with emotion she laughed. "I agree. Now is a great time to start our forever."

Brady placed the ring on her finger. His smile filled his face. "It is a great time."

Epilogue

Dear Dad,

I can't believe it's already been a year since you left us, and two years since I found out I was pregnant. So much has happened since you've been gone, and there's been so many times I wanted to talk to you, and it took me a second to remember that I can't. That you aren't with me. When Grant started walking, I caught myself looking for you, to laugh at his wobbliness with you, or when he said Mama for the first time—but you weren't there.

Two of my favorite pictures were taken without you even knowing about it, and the irony is, we didn't know it was going to be your last smile on camera, which makes them even more special. When we had our girls' weekend, and I Facetimed y'all. You were holding Grant. I caught a picture, which is now framed in his room. You are both looking at each other and have grins on your faces. The love you both shared for each other was so obvious. I want Grant to grow up remembering that look on your face, a look of admiration and love. There is also one of all three of you. You and Mom both cuddling Grant. I framed that and put it in his room as well. I am so glad I took those pictures. I cherish them, Dad.

I want you to know that I took your advice, and Brady and I have come a long way. You told me to listen to him and find it in my heart to forgive. It wasn't easy, Dad, but I finally did. Mom told me about your story, and it made me realize that beginnings are sometimes rocky, but if a life together is built on love, and both parties are willing to work hard, it will make it. Both Brady and I had some growing up to do, and things to ask for forgiveness for, but we decided that our love for each other was stronger than the challenges. That decision has led to today, and me writing this letter to you.

Dad, Brady and I are finally getting married. In just a few hours, I'll be walking down the aisle to join hands with the man I love, the daddy of my child, and become Mrs. Elizabeth Warren. We are getting married right here in our backyard, Dad. Just like we planned so long ago. The only thing that is missing, which is keeping this day from being the perfect wedding day of my dreams, is you. You aren't here to give me one of your powerful hugs, which always made me feel safe and gave me the courage to face whatever was troubling me. You aren't here to walk me down the aisle or kiss my cheek as you give me away. You aren't here to stand by Mom and hold her hand while she cries—and she will cry. But I know that you're here in my heart, and that has to be enough.

Everyone tells me that even though you aren't here in person, you are here in spirit. Grant has not only your name (Jackson Grant), but your smile, and there is a gleam in his eye when he is up to his two-year-old mischief, that Mom says reminds her of you. Oh, Dad, he loves football—I know, he's only two, but on Saturday's when Brady and I are in front of the TV, he is all engrossed, usually.

I love you so much, Dad. I promise you that I will stand by Brady, and love him, honor him, and cherish him, until death do us part—but like Mom, I will love him even after that, and I have no doubt he will do the same for me.

I wish I didn't have to end this letter, but I've got to get ready for my day, and my bridesmaids will be here soon—Jessica and Deb. We don't have a flower girl, but three mini ringbearers instead—say a prayer from above or send down an angel to rein them in—we'll need all the help we can get!

I love you so much—forever.

Your Lilly-Billy

Elizabeth folded the letter in half, tucking it in her purse for later, just as she heard Jessica and Deb enter the front door. Wiping her eyes, she got up from her desk and walked downstairs to eat breakfast and prepare for the morning. Hair, nails, makeup and finally dress.

"Lizzy, look at you!" Charlotte covered her face with her hands when she finally saw her daughter. She couldn't stop the tears from falling down her face as she wrapped Elizabeth in a tight hug. "You are the most beautiful bride."

Elizabeth sniffled. "Mom, please don't make me cry already. This makeup was expensive." She backed away from her mom and graciously accepted the tissue that Deb handed both her and her mother. Wiping her eyes, she started laughing as she watched her mom do the same. "It's gonna be one of those days, isn't it?"

Charlotte nodded, while gently wiping her eyes. "It is." She took a deep, calming breath and took in her daughter. Grown and standing before her. "Your dad would be so proud of the woman you've become. I know he's watching, and his joy is beaming down at you." Her eyes started filling up again.

"Mom..." Elizabeth's words were cut off as her voice caught in her throat, and she found herself having to fight her own tears.

"Both of you really need to stop. This isn't good for any of us." Jessica interrupted.

Elizabeth and her mom turned to see Jessica, Deb, and Joanna all dabbing lightly at their eyes to contain their tears before they dug paths in their made-up faces as well. Elizabeth moved all the women into a group and produced a large group hug, perfect for them to all contain themselves and pull themselves together.

"Thank you, everyone, for being a part of this day." Elizabeth looked around her circle at each face. "I'm so glad you're all here and can't wait to make our families come together. I love you and am so glad you've supported us from the beginning."

Christian poked his head in the door. "Hey, ladies, sorry to interrupt..." As they pulled away from each other, Christian got a good look at the bride and his eyes opened wide as a smile spread across his face. He came across the room to hug his soon-to-be sister-in-law. "You look absolutely stunning. My brother's going to flip when he sees you." He gave her a light kiss on the cheek. "But we have got to get this party started. We have three ring bearers, or whatever you're calling them, that are becoming rather bored and need to have something to do, and a groom who's needing his bride."

Charlotte gave her daughter an encouraging smile. "Okay, you ready?"

Elizabeth looked around at the women who she chose to share this day with, and Christian. Joy filled her heart, and a smile spread across her face. She took a deep breath and nodded. "Yes, I'm so ready for this."

Jessica and Deb gave her quick hugs as everyone headed down the stairs to take their place in the sunroom, where they were going to exit into the backyard.

Elizabeth watched through the windows as Brady's parents walked down the aisle, followed by her mom, the three ring bearers, and then Jessica and Deb. It was a perfect day for an outdoor wedding. The sun was high in the sky, with just a few scattered clouds. The flowers, daisies, Gerber daisies, black-eyed Susan's, all her and her father's favorites, were blooming in the garden. Birds gathered in the backyard, and a pair of cardinals at the bird feeder, chirping their songs of love.

She felt her father's presence as she left the door and entered her yard. She took a deep breath, smiled back at those amazing brown eyes waiting for her, and walked down the aisle toward him.

****

Elizabeth danced in the arms of her husband. Brady caressed her cheek, and they couldn't take their eyes off each other. Everything seemed different. The way Brady looked at her, the way she felt, his kisses. It all felt like she was in a dream, one in which she hoped would last forever. She was brought back to reality by a soft tug on her dress. She gazed down and became captivated by a tiny little person with soft brown curls and big brown eyes in a tiny tux. Leaning down, she picked Grant up, and Brady wrapped them both in his arms as they danced around the floor. Her heart was full. She was surrounded by the arms of her favorite boys, their love for her filling her heart as the music came to an end.

"Are you ready?" Brady looked at her with his calming gaze, leaned in to plant a soft kiss on her lips, but was pushed away by his little bitty competition. Smiling at Grant, he took his son from Elizabeth's arms. "Come on, buddy. We have another song to prepare for."

The family of three went to the microphone, as Elizabeth's

father's favorite song started playing on the speakers.

Elizabeth cleared her throat and looked around at her family and friends gathered to celebrate with them. She smiled out at the small crowd, found her mother, and took a deep breath.

"Hi, everyone. Thank you for coming." She paused and took another big breath, her mother's smile encouraging her. "The song you're hearing now is my dad's favorite. He always danced around the house to this song with me. I always told him it would be our song, the song I danced with him...." She took the tissue Brady offered her, and he wrapped his arm around her shoulders, giving her a squeeze of reassurance.

She let out a big breath. "Anyway, you all know how amazing a man he was... I... I wrote my dad a letter this morning. I want to read it to him, and then I want us to light some candles around the garden in his memory. He loved having just enough light out here in the yard at night to put a soft glow on everything. Anyway..."

She had to take a minute to compose herself and pulled the letter from her purse, which was sitting on the table next to them. Opening the letter and seeing the words she wrote brought new tears to her eyes. Grant pulled her to him in his little arms and wiped away one of the tears which had released itself from its corral. She smiled at her little man in his father's arms and leaned in to kiss him on his cheek. She felt a strength wash through her, took a deep breath, and read the words she wrote just hours before.

The birds' soft chirping was the only sound that could be heard when she finished reading the letter, and there wasn't a dry eye in the yard. Brady pulled her in, gave her a very soft, loving kiss, and wiped her face with a new tissue. "That was perfect."

Elizabeth smiled at him, laying her head on his shoulder, as Grant put his little hand on her face. She couldn't remember ever feeling this happy, this loved, this safe.

She closed her eyes and sent up a silent prayer. *Thank you, Dad, for making sure I listened to you. I love you.*

She smiled and put her arms around her boys.

Brady held her close. "I'll love you forever, Elizabeth."

And she knew it was the truth.

Acknowledgments

Book 2 is done! Wow!

It still surprises me that I am able to put my thoughts into words and make a town and characters come to life. I love Elizabeth, Jessica, Brady, Jacob, and everyone else in this little town. They have become part of my family. I cry when they cry and celebrate with them as well.

I wouldn't be able to do this, though, without the love and support of so many. Writing is not easy and takes a lot of my time, so I need to thank my husband for giving me the time I need to complete a manuscript, then the time it takes to go through the many revisions to make it better.

My friends and beta readers—Tonia, Cherie, and Sarah. You gave me feedback and your opinion, which altered the story and made it what it is today. Thank you.

My editors, proofreader, and cover designer/ formatter. This book wouldn't be possible without them.

And of course, my readers. You all are awesome. I hope you enjoy Brady and Elizabeth's journey and come back for more.

About the Author

Donna R. Madden is a mother of three and a wife of 30 years. She and her husband live in a small town north of Nashville. They share their house with their dog Lilly, and cat King Marcus Henry XXII, who they all affectionately call "Kitty Kitty." Their three boys are grown and out of the house, yet not out of their hearts. They are 27, 24, and 20. Yes, there will be a book focusing on three brothers one day.

Donna loves to tear through books any chance she can get. She loves romance and dystopian novels best, but she will read just about anything, and enjoys her job as a high school English teacher.

Outside of reading, she enjoys hanging out with her family and friends. She loves the great outdoors, the beach, and camping on their property in the hills of Kentucky.

Forever Enough is the continuation of Elizabeth's and Brady's journey.

Notes to the Reader

Thank you for taking your time and reading *Forever Enough,* in the *More Than Enough* series— the continuation of Elizabeth and Brady's story. I hope you enjoyed reading their story as much as I enjoyed writing it.

I know all of this book was not easy to read, but sometimes being together because of a baby is not enough to create a strong relationship. Brady and Elizabeth both needed to step back and really look at their relationship to see if it was what they really wanted. I am so glad they found a way to forgive and were able to find their love in each other. As you read on through the series, I hope you grow to love what they bring to the stories.

If you enjoyed reading this, I would be so grateful to you if you would take the time and leave a review for me. The more reviews authors have, the easier it is to find their books.

I love to hear from my readers, so please connect with me, on Instagram and Facebook-- Donna R. Madden Writer. Or email at drmaddenauthor@outlook.com

Made in the USA
Columbia, SC
24 February 2024